CRUISIN'

Lady Guardians

CELESTE GRANGER

Want to be in the know? Subscribe to my newsletter to be a part of Celeste Granger's Tangled Romance!
https://landing.mailerlite.com/webforms/landing/k2e1j4
Follow me on Facebook @ https://www.facebook.com/TheCelesteGranger/
Want to join my reading group, Reading with Celeste? Follow the link: https://www.facebook.com/groups/1943300475969127/

Acknowledgment

Here we are again! I cannot believe the incredible literary journey we've been on together, and the amazing support you've given me. I also would like to thank my graphic arts team, editors, and proofreaders. Thank you to my family and friends who continue to support my literary dreams. I love you!

This book is dedicated to those who are willing to let go of the past…
finally…

Chapter One

"Chica, is it going to always be like this now that you got a biker for a man?"

Carmen Rodriguez, Maitre'd at Café Laquette, stood near the front window with her hands on her curvy hips and her black patent leather stiletto rhythmically tapping the floor.

"What are you fussing about now," Onyx Malone asked, padding up alongside her sister-friend and long-time employee. The staff was cleaning up from Sunday brunch, so there were no customers in the restaurant at the time. Onyx looked out of the window and saw a row of four motorcycles and their riders, one of which she instantly recognized as the man of her dreams.

"Before, you would have stormed out of here and got them straight about parking in front of the restaurant," Carmen continued. "No mas, eh?"

Onyx barely heard what Carmen said. She was too busy watching Egypt Anderson, her fiancé, and president of the Dirty South Riders.

"That's how she got her man, Carmen, don't you remember," Tre' Jones asked. Tre' like Carmen, had been with Onyx since the beginning of Café Laquette. He was the café's head chef and resident big brother. Tre would as soon kick ass and take names, especially when it came to his girls, Onyx and Carmen.

"I know, I know," Carmen quipped, popping her lips and shifting her hips. "Still, they are practically blocking the door."

"Do you say that when me and the Lady Guardians roll up," Onyx asked, sliding her hand up her hip.

"Yes," Carmen clapped back. "You just don't hear me."

Onyx heard something else in Carmen's tone that caused Onyx to draw her attention back inside the space.

"What's really going on with you, Carmen," Onyx asked, trying to regain Carmen's attention as the maitre'd rolled her eyes.

Carmen's hands moved from her hips to folded across her ample chest. She popped her lips again and still avoided looking at Onyx.

"Carmen?" Onyx insisted. Now Tre' was staring at Carmen too, and she felt the unspoken pressure to respond.

"A Chica, no, quiero hablar de ello," Carmen rebuffed.

"You don't want to talk about it? Oh, we're talking about it," Onyx clapped back.

When Carmen stumped her foot, pouting like a three-year-old, Onyx tried not to laugh. Tre' did laugh, he couldn't help himself.

"I got another letter," Carmen groaned.

"From Juan Carlos," Onyx asked.

"Se, Juan Carlos," Carmen admitted.

"Ugh," Tre' groaned. "I'm outa here."

Carmen flipped her shoulder length jet black hair from her slender shoulder and pursed her lips as Tre' made his exit.

"What did he say this time that's different than the last sixteen thousand letters he's sent?" Onyx was instantly irritated by the whole thing.

"It hasn't been that many," Carmen sighed.

"But they all say the same thing, Carmen. I miss you, I love you. Wait for me."

Carme had nothing to say. Onyx was right, but that was beside the point.

"So is that why you're acting so stank," Onyx asked.

"What do you mean?" Carmen lifted an accusatory hand and pointed towards the window. "They are-"

"Don't try it, Carmen. Any other time the guys being out there doesn't bother you in the least. Explain why today it's such a big deal."

"El viene a casa," Carmen grumbled. Onyx vicariously learned Spanish from being around Carmen. She understood part of what Carmen said but wanted to make sure.

"What about your house?"

"No, not mi casa," Carmen fussed. El viene a casa. He's coming home!"

Onyx's eyes widened, and an unconscious hand moved to cover her open mouth.

"Girl, when?"

"Next month," Carmen moaned. Wrinkles creased Carmen's tawny brown flawless skin. Carmen was so caught up in emotional turmoil; she didn't notice one of the bikers checking for her. Grayson Foster, known to his biker buddies as Turks noticed Carmen before when Egypt and Onyx first got together. Turk thought Carmen was beautiful, exotically intriguing, but there just never seemed to be the right opportunity to introduce himself. He had hoped this time would be it.

"Damn," Onyx sighed. This wasn't the first time Juan Carlos said he was coming home. The other times, though, there was no time frame attached. This time, by the look on Carmen's face, she believed him this time.

"What are you going to do," Onyx asked, understanding her friend's disposition and genuinely concerned for her.

"I can't talk about this right now."

Carmen stormed off. Turk's eyes trailed her as she disappeared from view. Carmen's four-inch stilettos clicked rhythmically across the concrete floor. Onyx shook her head. She knew all too well what Juan Carlos' return or even the threat of his return meant for Carmen.

Carmen walked quickly past the line staff. She didn't want to talk to anyone. She couldn't, not right now. Dipping into Onyx's office, Carmen quickly closed the door behind her, not minding that it slammed. Her pace slowed as Carmen rounded the desk and sat heavily into the chair. It was all too much. As long as Juan Carlos was away, he was out of sight, out of mind. Carmen learned to prefer it that way. She'd grown, or at least she thought she had; until a letter arrived from Fulton Prison. That's when Carmen was thrust, kicking and screaming back into her past; a past she'd just as soon forget.

A RAP ON THE CAFÉ DOOR DREW ONYX'S ATTENTION FROM Carmen's situation. Turning toward the door, a smooth smile eased across Onyx's lips. There was a bit of sashay in her hips as she moved towards the door and opened it.

"Hey, beautiful," Egypt crooned, easing up to Onyx and kissing her lovingly on the cheek.

"Hey there, handsome," Onyx smiled. Her eyelashes fluttered as she blinked and breathed in. The smell of him made Onyx's heart smile.

"I had to stop by. I missed you," Egypt said as he stepped slightly back.

"You saw me this morning," Onyx laughed.

"That was a lifetime ago." Egypt extended his hands around Onyx's fine waist and eradicated any space between them. His lips found the succulence of her neck, and he nibbled her, sending Onyx into shrieks of giddiness. But she couldn't deny the pulsating heat that started in her core.

"You betta stop," Onyx giggled, looking around to see if anyone was there. Her body defied her, though, as she leaned into him, connecting with him, sending a current of heat to his essence.

"Do you really want me to?" Egypt trilled against the flesh of her neck sending a new wave of sensation to her jewel.

Onyx started fanning, and her face flushed. She playfully pushed Egypt away, as much for his sake as her own.

"Okay, okay," Egypt thrummed. "But promise we can pick up where we left off when you get home."

"About that," Onyx began. "It's Carmen."

"Is she okay?" Egypt asked, hearing the serious shift in Onyx's tone. The natural protector in Egypt rose up. He'd grown fond of Carmen. She was good people.

"News from her ex," Onyx sighed.

"The guy in jail?"

"Yep, that's the one," Onyx muttered. "He's getting out, soon. And she's totally bummed out. I may have to do a girl's night with her, try and cheer her up."

"Of course," Egypt answered. "Do what you need to, babe. Just call me and let me know you're okay."

"I promise," Onyx sighed. Lifting onto her tiptoes, Onyx kissed Egypt fully on the lips.

As she lowered herself, Egypt started to pedal backward. "Love ya."

Onyx smiled and flitted her fingers waving. "Love you, too."

Chapter Two

Carmen was doing more than sulking. There was sadness; a surprising melancholy. She thought she'd gotten past having any feelings for Juan Carlos, other than contempt. Yet, there she was, sitting behind Onyx's desk, with her head hung low. There was a painful familiarity to the weightiness Carmen felt. She'd experienced it many times before with Juan Carlos; when they were in love. Carmen had a propensity for the bad boys. She liked them edgy and macho, and Juan Carlos fit the bill perfectly... almost too perfectly. The two grew up in the same neighborhood. Carmen had known Juan Carlos since they were kids. He was a few years older and hung out with Carmen's older brothers. Even as kids, the girls thought Juan Carlos was cute. Carmen didn't see him that way. Besides, he treated her like a kid sister. By the time they were teenagers, the girls fawned all over him. He was no longer just cute, Juan was handsome. Where Carmen played it off before, the older she got, the harder it was to deny that there was something about him that she liked. He stopped treating her like a kid sister, in some ways. When her brothers would razz her, Juan Carlos would laugh along with them. But after they were out of eyesight, Juan would always check to make sure she was okay and then offer her a flashy smile.

It was that damn smile that melted Carmen's heart when she got older; old enough to have a boyfriend. Of course, her brothers didn't like the idea, even though Carmen was nearly twenty when she and Juan Carlos first got together. But their relationship was as much taboo as the two of them being related. Juan Carlos was her brothers' friend. He was family. Carmen should have been off limits. And her brothers insisted that she was. But Juan Carlos stood up to them and fought for their relationship. That's when Carmen knew Juan Carlos loved her. That's when she started overlooking the red flags.

Juan was her first. They were together for six years before he got locked up. Sitting back in the executive chair, Carmen shook her head and then she smiled; a wary smile. There was so much about their relationship that had been good. Juan Carlos had plenty of machismo. That was huge for Carmen. The men in her family were all strong, macho, proud men and she wanted nothing less from the man she loved. Juan Carlos was fiercely protective and jealous. If any guy even looked at Carmen too long, Juan Carlos was ready to go to blows. In the beginning, Carmen thought it was cute, and the right thing for a boyfriend to do. But it started to get out of hand. His protection of her became possession. Juan Carlos became increasingly demanding; insistent on knowing where she went, who she was with, how long she'd be gone and when she'd be back. It started to feel like too much. Yet, Carmen's young love for Juan Carlos wouldn't let her see the truth.

It wasn't until Juan Carlos was incarcerated that Carmen started to see things clearly. The rose-tinted glasses were forcibly removed in his unexpected absence. Still, Juan had a hold on her. He had a stranglehold on Carmen's heart, and he reinforced it every time she visited. "You're my girl. You belong to me.' Carmen scoffed, now. Those words used to be music to her ears. She would answer with a resounding yes, promising that he was the only man for her, that she would be faithful to him no matter how long it took. And she was. Carmen visited Juan Carlos every week, faithfully, that first year of his incarceration. The letters came, between visits and Carmen wrote him back, every single time; even when there was nothing much to say. She held true to her promise. The second year, she didn't visit quite as much, and the hold he had on her started to dissipate. Part of it was Carmen maturing, moving out of the neighborhood and seeing other things, meeting other people. The other part of it was meeting Onyx.

The two women hit it off immediately. They were so different, coming from different backgrounds, and having different life experiences. Onyx was smart, independent, goal driven. Carmen was intelligent, as well. But her only goal was to become a good wife to a decent man. Being independent, for Carmen, was contrary to everything Carmen had been taught about a woman's place in the world. But their differences didn't seem to matter. Carmen and Onyx had enough in common that they became fast friends. Their relationship helped to change Carmen's perspective, not only regarding romantic love but self-love. The more Carmen got to know herself, her worth, the less she was enchanted by Juan Carlos. After a while, she no longer felt compelled to visit or to write back. But that didn't stop the stupid letters from coming. They came like clockwork, and even though Carmen thought she was emotionally unattached to him, she read every word…still…

That's the part that made Carmen feel sick to her stomach, even as she sat in Onyx's office. Carmen's stomach had been in knots since she read those fateful words. "I'm coming home to you, soon."

"Ugh…"

"Still feeling blue," Onyx asked as she peeked her head inside the door. Carmen had been so lost in her own thoughts, she hadn't heard Onyx tap on the door, or open it, for that matter. When Carmen looked up, Onyx did her best to suppress the giggle threatening to escape her lips. Carmen had the cutest lil pouty look on her face. Her lower lip was poked out, and her shoulders were slumped over.

"Muy azul," Carmen moaned. "Very, very blue…"

"Aw," Onyx sighed, walking over to the desk and sitting on the corner. "Let's get out of here, do something to take your mind off your cellmate."

"That is so not funny, Onyx! Pendejo tonto del culo que te jodan gillipollas. Chingados, Onyx, Chingados!"

"Okay, okay, my bad," Onyx said apologetically, doing her best to keep a straight face. She didn't understand all of it, but Onyx understood enough to know that what she said pissed Carmen off. The puppy dog sad face was gone. Carmen was on her feet, and once again her hands were folded across her chest. *At least that's something*, Onyx thought to herself as she tried to appease her friend.

"So, does that mean we can have a girl's night out?" Onyx persisted.

"I don't feel like it," Carmen groaned. "I'm too upset."

"Come on, Carmen. Okay, we don't have to go out. We can go back to your place, pop some popcorn, drink some wine, eat some ice cream and watch all your favorite reruns.

Carmen paused giving it some thought.

"Your place is nicer than mine," she bemoaned.

"Okay, my place then," Onyx corrected.

"I don't know," Carmen reconsidered. "Maybe I'll just go home, be by myself, sulk in private, you know?"

"No ma'am," Onyx insisted. "We are hanging out whether you like it or not." Onyx got up from the desk and walked behind Carmen, gently pushing her, compelling Carmen's stubborn feet towards the door.

"I promise you'll feel better," Onyx said, reassuringly.

"You promise?"

CARMEN KICKED OFF HER SHOES AND PULLED HER HAIR UP IN A messy bun atop her head. She flopped down on the couch, waiting for Onyx to return with the wine and popcorn, but more so the wine. The television was on, but Carmen could scarcely pay attention. All she kept thinking about was the calendar and how many more days of freedom she had. If Juan Carlos was anything like he used to be or anything like he promised to be, Carmen knew that the first thing he would do is come looking for her. He assumed, even after nearly ten years behind bars, that they were still together. His letters as much as said so. Carmen hadn't had the heart to respond to the letters let alone tell him that she'd moved on. And she had; at least Carmen tried.

She dated other guys after Juan Carlos' first three years of incarceration. But there were two problems: initially she felt guilty about dating someone other than Juan Carlos; and secondly, Carmen found herself picking the same kind of guy to date. Sure, the guys had different names, and even came from different neighborhoods. However, underneath it all, they were the same kind of obsessive, possessive machismo who felt the need to control Carmen, practically from the very beginning. Carmen had a type, and after several failed dates and a few failed short-term relationships, Carmen resigned herself to focus on something other than her love life.

Receiving that letter brought it all back to the forefront.

Onyx reentered the room and sat on the couch next to Carmen. The wine glasses were already on the table, and Onyx poured a healthy serving of the Pinot Noir into Carmen's glass at her behest.

"So, what all did the letter say," Onyx asked taking a sip of the wine.

"I already told you, he's getting out," Carmen sighed. She took a long sip of the wine and then reached for the bottle to refill her glass.

"I get the feeling there was more to it than that," Onyx replied.

"Oh, you mean the part where he said he still loved me, and his intention was for us to be together and that he would never let me go. You mean, that part?"

"Yeah, that part," Onyx replied. "I'll get the ice cream. Mint chocolate chip or rocky road?"

"Both."

Carmen rested her head on the back of the couch. Normally, she tried to be upbeat and happy. She was happy with her life as it was. Being the second in command at her best friend's very popular restaurant, having great friends, and her family had been enough. Having Juan Carlos reappear would drag her back to a past that she would just as soon forget.

Onyx reemerged with two quarts of ice cream and four spoons. Carmen lifted her head long enough to grab the mint chocolate chip and a spoon. She left the lid on the table as she spooned the ice cream and rested her head back on the couch.

"I take it you've never told him you're no longer interested?"

"I tried, un montón de veces. I started to let him in a letter, but I just couldn't bring myself to mail it."

"No wonder he thinks he has a chance, Carmen. You never told him he didn't," Onyx commented. "He doesn't, does he?"

Carmen lifted up with the spoon balanced upside down in her mouth. She pulled it out slowly as her eyes tightened. "Uh, no, he doesn't."

"But does he know that," Onyx asked.

"He should, Carmen replied.

"That's my point though, Carmen," Onyx continued. "From what he wrote in the letter, it doesn't sound like Juan Carlos has a clue."

"Then he needs to go on that show where the lady spins the letters and buy a damn vowel. Punta!"

Onyx had to cover her mouth to keep her ice cream from splaying.

"No, what you need to do is tell him, before he gets out… with emphasis on the before."

Carmen's head fell back between her shoulders and a slow groan passed through her lips.

"You know I'm right."

I just don't think I can face him again," Carmen answered, returning her gaze to her friend.

"Either you face him in there, or he shows up at your door. You choose."

"This is not helping me," Carmen huffed.

"I'm sorry, babe, but seriously, you can't let Juan Carlos control your life. You've gotta tell him."

Just then Onyx's phone chirped to life.

"Dangit, I forgot to call Egypt." The phone chirped again. "Sorry, girl. I'll just be a minute."

Onyx got up from the couch and went into another room to answer her phone.

Carmen knew Onyx was right. Still, she couldn't imagine going back to that prison. It didn't take much to remember how the bars clanged when the doors slammed or that awful lack of fresh air smell. The place felt like hopelessness if being hopeless had a feeling. It was enough to give anyone the creeps.

"I'm so sorry, totally escaped my mind," Onyx began after their greeting salutations. "Carmen and I came back to the house and started talking."

"No worries, babe, as long as you ladies are okay," Egypt answered.

"So, where are you?"

"Turks and I just came from checking out the new property seeing the progress the crew was making. We were just about to stop by the house and go over the architectural plans, but since you ladies are there," Egypt contended.

"I don't want you to have to change your plans," Onyx replied. "Hold on one sec." Onyx moved in with Egypt after they got engaged earlier in the year. His home was now her home, too.

Onyx's voice sound muffled like she had her hand over the speaker.

"Carmen, Egypt, and Turks were on their way over. Do you mind? They'll stay out of our way, promise."

"It doesn't matter either way," Carmen bemoaned.

"Never mind. I feel bad for asking. I promised you a girls' night."

"It's cool," Carmen answered.

"Are you sure?" Onyx asked.

"I've got ice cream, wine, and a comfy couch. It's fine." Carmen offered Onyx a slight smile. Not being alone in her own thoughts was really all Carmen needed. She appreciated Onyx for being a listening ear.

"Come on home, babe," Onyx said.

"Alright, see you soon."

"Not soon enough," Onyx smiled.

Egypt and Turks entered through the kitchen door.

Instinctually, Onyx turned around hearing the sound.

"Go get your man," Carmen replied. "I'm going to the ladies' room."

Onyx and Carmen got up at the same time, one headed toward the restroom and one headed toward the kitchen.

"Hey babe," Egypt said with a smile as she entered.

"Turks, how are you doing?"

"I'm good, Onyx."

"Hey handsome," Onyx purred as she walked into Egypt's open arms. Turks knew Carmen was there because Egypt mentioned it on the ride over. He hoped she'd be coming into the kitchen as well and looked toward the door in anticipation. Turks looked back over his shoulder seeing Egypt and Onyx cuddled up. He started to say that he was going to the restroom but figured they wouldn't notice he was gone, not initially. Turks strode from the kitchen down the hallway. When the door to the restroom opened, he paused as light spilled into the hallway. His hooded eyes smiled when Carmen stepped through the door.

Turks immediately noticed the difference in the way Carmen moved. He'd seen her confident, sexy stride before. This wasn't it. She didn't even look up as she drew closer to him. Still, he couldn't take his eyes off her.

"Hey," Turks crooned as Carmen got closer.

"Oh hey," Carmen replied, barely looking up.

"You okay," Turks asked turning slightly as she passed.

"No," Carmen admitted finally pausing and looking up. Turks was immediately drawn in by her exquisite beauty, even though her eyes were sad.

"I'm sorry to hear that," Turks answered, trying not to stare. "Is there anything I can do to help?"

"No, but thanks for asking. I've got wine and ice cream." Carmen offered a smile. Turks noticed that her smile didn't reach her eyes.

"I'm Turks, Grayson, by the way." He extended an upturned hand.

"Carmen," she replied, accepting Turks hand. His grip was firm yet gentle.

"It's nice to finally meet you," Turks crooned. "I just wish the circumstances were different. Feel better, okay?"

"Thanks, Grayson."

He held her hand a little longer and then watched as Carmen turned and padded down the hallway.

By the time Carmen got to the living room, Onyx was there waiting for her.

"Are you feeling any better?"

Carmen sat down next to her and tucked her feet underneath. "Some," Carmen replied. "Met a fine man in your hallway though, so that's something."

"That was Turks. You think he's fine," Onyx smiled.

"I'm sad, Chica, not blind," Carmen quipped.

"Ah, mmhmm," Onyx replied. She was glad to see a little of Carmen's fire coming back. "You've seen him before," Onyx continued. "He was one of the bikers you complained about earlier today."

"I was sadder then," Carmen sighed.

"Mmhmm."

Egypt and Turks were downstairs, drinking cognac and looking over the architectural plans for the newest installment in the Anderson Project. Turks had been a part of Egypt's company since its inception; before Anderson Construction became a multimillion-dollar enterprise. Not only were they bike brothers, but the two had also been friends for a long time before that, going back to their college days. Egypt knew Turks to be an incredible architect and overall a good dude. He trusted Turks with his life.

"What do you think about adding an additional acre to the premium plots," Egypt asked. His eyes were downcast, looking at the plans. When there was no response from Turks, Egypt looked up.

"Hey bro, did you hear me?"

"Huh, yeah. Sounds good," Turks replied indifferently.

Egypt stood up and regarded his friend. "You didn't hear a word I said. What's up, man? Your focus has been off since we came downstairs."

"I'm good," Turks replied, "let's keep going." Turks turned up the drink he held in his hand and downed it. He started to look at the plans again.

"Naw, let's talk about what has you so preoccupied," Egypt insisted.

Turks dropped his head and shook it slightly.

"I ran into Carmen," he admitted.

"Oh, okay," Egypt smiled. "Now we're getting to it."

Turks turned and leaned against the table. Egypt laughed at Turks trying not to smile. "I don't know man, it's just something about her."

"I know how that is," Egypt answered. "It was the same way for me the first time I saw Onyx." Egypt smiled just thinking about it.

"Did you step to Carmen?"

"We spoke," Turks replied. "It wasn't an ideal situation though."

"Then do something about it," Egypt encouraged. "It's obvious you like her."

A few hours later

ONYX AND EGYPT LAY SNUGGLED IN THEIR BED; HIS ARM draped lovingly around her waist.

"Carmen feeling any better?"

"Not really," Onyx replied as she rubbed the back of Egypt's hand. "She's resting in the guest bedroom."

"Hate to hear she's not feeling well, but she certainly made Turks night."

Onyx turned her head to face him. "Really?"

"Yeah," Egypt smiled. "Turks couldn't even focus after he ran into her."

"Really," Onyx asked again. Now she was smiling.

"Turks could be just what Carmen needs to get over Juan Carlos," Onyx mused.

"Who's Juan Carlos?"

"Carmen's tainted past," Onyx replied. "That's a story for another day. But maybe you and I can help Turks be her future?"

"Ah, we can do that," Egypt replied. "Should we though?"

Onyx turned fully to face Egypt. She gently stroked the side of his face as she spoke. "If we have an opportunity to play even a small role in two people who deserve love actually finding what we have, babe, we have an obligation to assist."

"And what exactly do we have," Egypt trilled, tickling Onyx's ear.

"Love, baby. We have incredible, beautiful, earth-shattering love," Onyx purred.

"Mmm," Egypt moaned as he leaned in, capturing Onyx's full lips with his own.

"Then who are we to deny our friends the same?"

Chapter Three

Onyx ad Egypt wasted no time in setting up the non-accidental encounter for Carmen and Turks. The girls were going over the books after Friday night dinner service.

"I don't know if this is such a good idea, Onyx," Carmen replied. "He's cute and all, but I don't think I'm in the right head space."

"Why not, Carmen? Anything to take your mind off, Mr. Incarcerated."

"Oh, so you got jokes? ¿Crees que eres gracioso, hoy?"

Onyx laughed. "Come on, Carmen. Don't think about it as a date. It'll be the four of us. Do it for me, pleaassse?"

Now Onyx was the one with the turned down lips, batting her eyes and doing her best to look sad.

"Fine, multa," Carmen gave in.

"Squee! Thank you," Onyx exclaimed reaching over and hugging Carmen around the neck. "It's gonna be awesome."

"It better be."

The environment was familiar and comfortable; the perfect backdrop for what Egypt and Onyx hoped would be a great space for Turks and Carmen to make a real connection. They hired world class Chef Andre to come into their home for a communal cooking session.

"Do I look okay," Carmen asked for the third time in as few minutes.

"For someone who wasn't interested, you sure are concerned about how you look," Onyx quipped.

"Silencio, por favor," Carmen muttered.

"I'll hush," Onyx laughed. "But you're excited."

Just then the doorbell rang. Carmen's hands immediately went to her stomach.

"He's here," Onyx grinned. "Are you ready?"

"Oh my God," Carmen whined. "My stomach! The butterflies or something. I feel queasy." Carmen paused as she rubbed her belly. "Maybe this isn't such a good idea."

Egypt went to the door and answered it.

"What's up, man?"

"All good," Turks replied, giving Egypt some dap. "Is she here?"

"Yeah man, Carmen's here. Come on in."

Egypt led Turks into the kitchen, and the men got settled in. Turks was nervous, too. There was a tightness in his stomach. He did his best not to show it. After a few minutes, the ladies entered.

Both men stood up as they entered.

"Turks, this is Carmen Rodriguez, officially," Onyx said.

Carmen stepped forward, smoothing out her hair. Turks stepped forward as well.

"Nice to see you again, Carmen."

They shook hands again, and their eyes connected. An easy smiled moved across Turks lips, and Carmen smiled in return.

"Good to see you, too, Grayson."

"And this is Chef Andre. He's going to be teaching us how to cook," Egypt added.

"Shall we get started?" Chef Andre asked.

"Let's," Onyx replied.

"Fantastic," Andre answered. "There are aprons for each of you."

Turks took a slight step back and extended his hand for Carmen to pass in front of him. He secured his apron first.

"Let me help you with that," Turks suggested.

"I think I can manage," Carmen answered. Maybe it was the butterflies doing somersaults in her belly, or maybe it was from trying to play it cool; all the while feeling her knees knock together, but whatever the reason, Carmen couldn't get her fingers to cooperate with tying the apron behind her. Turks watched Carmen as he secured his own apron. He saw her fiddling and fumbling, doing her best to do it herself. When she sighed loud enough for Turks to hear, he stepped forward again.

"Let me help you with that," Turks suggested again. Carmen acquiesced.

"Sure."

She felt heat rising in her cheeks as Turks stepped forward. She turned her back to him and flushed warmer as he gently eased her hair from her shoulder. Turks tied the bow behind her neck and then carefully tied the bow at her waist. He noticed the curve of her waist and the voluptuousness of

Carmen's hips. Spinning on her heels, Carmen turned to face him.

"Thank you."

Their eyes connected, and Turks held her with a soft yet intense gaze. Carmen felt the butterflies again. She didn't want to feel what she felt. She didn't want to feel weak to him. Carmen didn't even know Turks really.

"You're welcome."

They walked together to the kitchen island, standing side by side. Carmen breathed in deeply, trying to quiet her nerves. In doing so, she took in his scent; understated yet distinctively pleasing.

"I don't know what Onyx and Egypt told you, but this is going to be an interactive lesson, from the selection of the wine through meal preparation," Andre said. "We're going to do an appetizer, Caesar salad, pasta for the main course and we're even having dessert. So, let's get started with the wine."

Chef Andre ensured everyone had a wine glass, as he continued.

"Malbec or Cabernet Sauvignon are excellent accompaniments to the meal we're going to prepare. This is one of my favorites, the 2016 Caymus Voyage Red Schooner."

Chef Andre took the liberty of pouring a sip into each glass.

"Most people don't appreciate wine. They don't take the time to savor the layers of flavor that compromise an exquisite wine. Now, each of you, take a moment and swirl the wine in the glass. Doing so should give you an appreciation for the color. It also helps to mix the flavors so that one is not more prominent than the other."

The couples did as the chef suggested. Carmen felt eyes on her. Her skin felt warm from his penetrating gaze, and she smiled. When she looked up, Turks was swirling his glass, but his eyes were elsewhere.

"What?" Carmen whispered finding it difficult to erase the grin from her lips.

Turks gaze held, and he saw the hint of gold in Carmen's eyes. He leaned his six-foot frame down to meet her much shorter frame and moved close to Carmen's ear so only she could hear him.

"The right thing to say is, forgive me for staring. I'm going to have to keep apologizing for this, and I'm okay with that as long as you don't get tired of hearing it. I can't help staring, though. You are stunning."

The feel of his warm breath against her skin sent an unexpected tingle through Carmen. She crossed her legs at the ankle, pulling her thighs together as the sensation resonated in her core. It was a feeling Carmen hadn't had in that way in longer than she could remember, if ever.

"I bet you've said that to a lot of women," Carmen countered.

Turks pulled back, so he could look Carmen in the eyes as he replied.

"No, you're the first."

Carmen pulled back. Her natural predilection was to return his comment with sass. But when she looked in Turks eyes, she didn't get the sense that he was reciting a well-played line. His eyes matched his tone. Carmen read genuineness there. Another unexpected. When she turned away from Turks to force herself to focus on what the chef was saying, a smile played on Carmen's lips. She looked across the island and saw Onyx wearing a wide grin. Carmen wanted to cross her eyes or stick out her tongue, but she didn't. Turks may see that. Instead, Carmen narrowed her eyes, and the corner of her lips turned slightly up. Onyx snickered. She knew what that nonverbal communication from her bestie meant.

"Now, let's lift the glass to your nose and smell the bouquet. What layers do you smell? Is there one scent more powerful than the other?"

Again, the couples followed suit, each lifting the glass to their nose and inhaling deeply.

"What do you smell," Turks raised the question with Carmen. Turning to face him, Carmen lifted the glass again; taking a slow deep inhale. And when she looked up over the glass, she looked directly into Turks compelling eyes. Her resolve was waning, whether Carmen liked it or not.

"Hmm," she hummed as her lashes fluttered. "I smell citrus, citricos jugosos, juicy citrus." Carmen's eyes smiled as much as her lips.

"Anything else," Turks chortled. Carmen placed her nose close to the rim of the glass again.

"Yes, there's something else, something sweet but I don't know," Carmen replied. "What do you smell, Grayson?"

Turks liked how she said his name; how it rolled off her sultry lips.

Turks lowered his eyes and lifted the glass. Carmen watched as his nostrils slightly flared when he inhaled, and she was there when his dark, brooding eyes found her again.

"Savory," he whispered. "Something woodsy with a hint of herbs."

Carmen giggled. "You have a good nose, Hermoso."

"Hermoso?"

"Hermoso, handsome," Carmen flirtatiously translated.

"You think I'm handsome," Turks asked, leaning in.

Before Carmen could answer, the chef spoke again.

"And lastly, let's taste the wine."

The heat rising in Carmen's cheeks and the sweet smile that infiltrated Carmen's lips wasn't missed by an observant Turks.

Onyx nudged Egypt as discretely as she could. She hadn't taken her eyes off Turks and Carmen since their introduction. Onyx turned to Egypt and smiled.

All the reservations Carmen had about spending time with Grayson started to fade into the background. Carmen smiled, realizing she hadn't thought about Juan Carlos since she entered the room. He had been her pervasive thought since receiving the letter. Yet, over the course of the time, she'd been in Turks presence, Carmen hadn't thought about him once. That was a good thing.

Meal preparation was just as enticing and electrically charged as the tasting of the wine had been. By the time the chef completed his instructions, the couples had a delicious meal they'd prepared themselves. The setting in the dining room was inviting and romantic, with fresh flowers providing beautiful aromatics and lit candles offering soft ambient light.

"You ladies have worked hard enough," Egypt suggested as he and Turks assisted the ladies in sitting down at the table. "Turks and I will bring in the food."

"Well, that's awful nice of you, honey," Onyx purred.

"It's the least I can do," Egypt strummed, leaning in and kissing Onyx lightly on the forehead.

As Turks and Egypt strode out of the room, Onyx gained Carmen's attention.

"So, it's going well, huh?" Onyx asked with a knowing smile dancing on her lips.

"Meh, asi asi," Carmen quipped.

"Just so so," Onyx challenged. "You are such a liar right now!" Onyx responded louder than she intended as she didn't want the guys to hear, but still, she didn't believe Carmen for one minute. And when Carmen turned away from Onyx trying to hide a smile, Onyx knew she hadn't misread the energy she'd seen between the two.

"Liar, liar pants on fire," Onyx hissed as she heard the men returning. Carmen didn't hide her smile anymore and hit Onyx with a quick wink as Egypt and Turks entered the room.

Carmen's eyes moved from Onyx to Turks as his powerful frame confidently glided in her direction. As Turks leaned down, placing the plate on the table, Carmen inhaled slowly, as the hint of his masculine scent filled her nose. Her feminine proclivities were titillated whether Carmen dared to admit it or not. Turks sat down next to her. Still his scent, his essence penetrated her senses more than the food in front of her. During dinner, the conversation was light, and then it took an unexpected turn.

"Carmen, tell me something about you that no one else knows," Turks asked, flirtatiously challenging Carmen to be honest.

"Is this what you guys call verdad o reto," Carmen purred. When she saw Turks didn't fully understand her response, she clarified for him. "Uhm, truth or dare?"

"Oh, no," Turks laughed. "Just making conversation," he acquiesced.

"No Papi," Carmen rebuffed. "No te creo. I don't believe you."

"And why is that," Turks chortled, taking a moment to dab the corners of his mouth while partially cloaking his emerging smile.

"Because, Grayson, you are an intentional man. Your questions have a purpose, never random or just conversational."

"Is that what you think of me," Turks asked.

"The better question is, what do you think of me?"

Carmen's dark eyes held him captive, and Grayson didn't back down from the intensity of her stare. She was dangerous, daring. Grayson was even more intrigued.

"So, no answer, sin repuesta?" The curve of her lip and the arch of her brow drew Grayson in deeper.

"I have an answer to your question, beautiful. But I would rather share it with you later, privately, when you go out with me."

"Hmm," Carmen hummed.

"Which makes the assumption that I am interested in seeing you again."

"Aren't you," Turks countered.

Chapter Four

After such a long night at Onyx and Egypt's, Carmen was dragging when she arrived to work the next day. Patrons were already standing in line waiting for the doors of Café Laquette to open for lunch. Onyx noticed Carmen not being her normal, perky self, eager to greet the customers and charged by the crazy rush of energy restaurant life provided.

"What? You can't hang, Chica?" Onyx teased as she smiled and greeted the customers.

"I can hang," Carmen sighed, doing her best to put on a smile as customers waited in line for her to seat them.

"Doesn't look like it," Onyx taunted. Their conversation was abbreviated as the demand from the café's patrons increased. They had already waited in line to come in. Onyx made sure they didn't wait unnecessarily to be served.

"So, what's the problem," Onyx asked during a momentary break in service.

"I didn't sleep well," Carmen answered. Onyx could see preoccupation; not just from the reservations Carmen reviewed, but also from the distant look in her eyes.

"Juan Carlos again?"

"Why do you have to say it like that? Vamos dame un

respire! Please, give me a break!"

"Okay, you and me in the back," Onyx insisted discretely taking Carmen by the arm.

"Renee, can you take over for Carmen for a minute?"

"Sure, Ms. Malone," the assistant maitre'd replied.

Carmen had to walk quickly to keep up with Onyx's march to the back of the house. Onyx didn't stop until they were behind closed doors.

"What is going on with you?" Onyx asked finally releasing the hold she had on her friend.

"Nothing, everything!" Carmen replied, sitting heavily down in the set across from Onyx's desk.

"Talk to me, Carmen. What's up?"

"I didn't mean to snap at you, seriamente," Carmen answered apologetically.

"That tells me nothing," Onyx countered as she leaned against the desk and folded her arms across her chest.

"Maybe I'm just tired," Carmen offered. "I didn't sleep well last night."

"I'll ask again. Is it because of Juan Carlos?"

"No," Carmen insisted. "And yes, I don't know."

Carmen crossed her legs and pushed her long black hair from her shoulders. She was irritated. Onyx could see that. But there was more to it than just irritation. Onyx had no intention of letting Carmen off the hook until she fessed up.

"You do understand that we are not leaving this room until you tell me what's going on."

"I know that," Carmen hissed. "That's why I'm so aggravated."

"Your frustration is not with me, Carmen."

"I know that, too," Carmen whined. Now Carmen's arms were folded across her chest, and her left foot bounced rhythmically atop her right as her pouting session continued. When that failed to satisfy her, Carmen lifted herself from the chair and began pacing on her four-inch stilettoes. Onyx waited her out. She knew that at some point, the pacing would stop, and the conversation would continue. Onyx tried not to laugh, as Carmen cursed in Spanish under her breath. Carmen was so animated, pacing faster and flailing her hands as a string of profanities that needed no translation spilled from her lips.

"Got it all out now," Onyx snickered, finding it hard to keep it together.

"I think so," Carmen murmured as she crossed the office and regained her seat.

"It's clear you don't want to talk about the incarcerated one whose name I won't mention." Carmen rolled her eyes as Onyx continued. "So, let's change the subject. Let's talk about Turks," Onyx suggested smilingly.

"What about him?"

"What do you mean, what about him? Carmen, you looked like you were having such a great time with Turks last night. I fully expected you to come in this morning, floating on a happy cloud of new possibilities. But, nooooo! You're all, I don't know."

"Frustrated?" Carmen suggested

"Yes!"

"Uptight?" Carmen sassed.

"Hell yes!" Onyx quipped.

"Irritating?"

"That's a definite, hell yes!" Onyx laughed.

"It's not funny," Carmen moaned.

"Did he do something wrong?"

"No," Carmen replied. "He asked me out."

"And that's a problem because…"

"Because," Carmen sang. "Can we go back to work now? I promise I'm feeling better."

"Nope," Onyx quipped.

A heavy sigh passed through Carmen's lips. She wasn't even sure how she was feeling let alone be able to make it make sense to someone else.

"He was nice, attentive, funny," Carmen reluctantly admitted. "I give him that."

"I am struggling to find the problem with that," Onyx replied.

"Me too," Carmen admitted. "That's the problem."

"Oh, so my instincts were right. You do like him."

"But I'm not supposed to," Carmen confessed.

Onyx shifted her position, squatting down in front of Carmen.

"Oh Carmen, honey, don't do that to yourself. Hell, don't let the imprisoned one do that to you either."

Carmen lifted her head, and her eyes met Onyx's. In Carmen's head, she knew Onyx was right. It was her own heart Carmen struggled with.

"I'm trying," Carmen affirmed. "I really am."

Onyx knew that's all she could really ask of Carmen. Pushing her would be counterproductive.

"Can we go back to work now? I need to think about something else."

"Sure," Onyx replied. "Let's get back to work."

Carmen's traipse to the front of the restaurant was much faster than her retreat. The bustle of the customers was exactly what Carmen needed to take her mind off her own issues. Near the end of the lunch rush, Carmen was in the zone, back to her regular gregarious self. Shutting off her thoughts, her real emotions made that possible. Carmen was actually feeling pretty good as she checked the reservations for the evening's dinner. The rumbling of a motorcycle just outside the front window drew Carmen's attention. She was fully prepared to fuss at Onyx about her man showing up again. However, when Carmen looked up, it wasn't Egypt on the back of the bike. It was Grayson.

Carmen watched Grayson as he balanced the heavy bike between his strong thighs. She wanted to look away. It was the right thing to do. But she couldn't as she felt his eyes find her even through the glass of the window pane. Carmen felt color rise in her cheeks as heat flushed through her core. Carmen turned away as Grayson's probative gaze became too much. Suddenly, the reservation list became much more interesting.

When the front door opened, Carmen's natural predilection was to look up. But even before she did, Carmen knew precisely who it was. She felt him before she saw him. A part of her essence responded to his presence.

"Table for one, please," his throaty baritone voice crooned.

Carmen's mink lashes batted as she lifted her head coming face to face with him.

"Dining alone?"

"Not if you decide to join me," Turks cruised.

"You don't stop, do you?" Carmen asked.

"Not until I get what I want," Turks answered. A mischievous line lingered at the corners of his mouth.

"And does that happen often? That you get what you want," Carmen inquired, trying to avoid staring at Turks luscious lips. She didn't even realize she had folded her lips in and slowly released them as her eyes remain transfixed on his. But Turks noticed, and so did the carnal nature of his flesh.

Always," Turk crooned.

Carmen's eyes narrowed as she sized Grayson up. Picking up a menu, Carmen sauntered around the pedestaled stand she stood behind. Once she was a few paces in front of him, and sure Turks was watching her ass, she paused, flipping her luxurious hair over her shoulder.

"Follow me."

The salaciousness in her tone was not lost on Turks, and Carmen did catch him looking at her ass. A smile eased across his lips as he strolled behind her, mesmerized by the natural sway of her hips and the firm of her thighs. Carmen found a table for Turks by the window.

"This way you can keep your eyes on your bike," Carmen purred. "Isn't that what biker's love, their motorcycles?"

"I take it you're not a fan of bikers, or maybe you don't like bikes," Turks queried.

"Bikes are fine, noisy but fine," Carmen replied. "Bikers? No lo se."

"Translate for me," Turks requested, leaning forward in his seat, closing the distance between them.

"No lo se means, I don't know," Carmen replied; being careful to enunciate every syllable of each word.

"Would you like to know," Turks mused.

"Know? About what?" Carmen countered.

"Whether you like bikers," Turks answered.

When you join me, beautiful, I can keep my eyes on you."

"Who said I was joining you," Carmen asked, sliding her hand to rest on her ample hip.

"You will," Turks countered, lowering his tall frame to the chair.

Carmen sat the menu down on the table in front of Grayson without pausing before sashaying away. Turks eyes barely grazed the menu. Although he knew the food at the café to be good, food is not what Turks was interested in. Carmen returned to her station and tried to focus on the work in front of her. There were a few lunch customers remaining in the restaurant. Carmen made it her business to ensure all their needs were met and they were satisfied with their culinary experience before leaving. Wherever she moved around the café, she knew Grayson was watching her.

"Ahnn," Onyx chimed. "He must really like you."

"Why do you say that?" Carmen asked innocently while feeling Grayson's eyes on her in his periphery.

"Because he hasn't taken his eyes off you since he sat down."

"That doesn't mean anything," Carmen replied dismissively.

"That, my dear, means everything," Onyx insisted. As Onyx walked away, Carmen considered what she'd said. Carmen watched as the last of the patrons exited the restaurant. The only one who remained was Grayson. It wasn't uncommon for staff to take a break and have an early dinner before the next onslaught of customers arrived. Carmen wasn't surprised when Tre', the head chef, emerged from the back of the house followed by the rest of the line staff. The kitchen crew brought out trays of the café's most popular dishes. The waitresses pushed the tables together, so the crew could dine together.

"Carmen Santiago," Tre' called out across the room. "You coming, boo?"

Under ordinary circumstances, Carmen would join the rest of the team for dinner. She tried to signal him from the maitre'd stand, darting her eyes in Grayson's direction and then looking back at Tre'. But he was too far away to read her nonverbal cues. When she didn't immediately respond, Tre' crossed the room to find out what was going on. Carmen still tried to clue him in, while avoiding making direct eye contact with Grayson.

"What, are you not hungry? Are you sick or something?" Tre' demanded.

Carmen grabbed Tre' by the arm and turned her back so that they could have a private conversation.

"Do you see that guy sitting by the window?"

"What guy," Tre' asked starting to turn around.

"No! Don't let him see you looking," Carmen hissed, pinching Tre's

arm even tighter.

"Ouch girl! You know I have sensitive skin," Tre' fussed.

"Just don't let him see you looking, okay," Carmen reasoned.

"Fine," Tre' acquiesced, pulling his arm from Carmen's clutches and rubbing the place where she held him. Tre' did get a look at the man by the window. He was almost unavoidable.

"I thought all the customers were gone. This is our time," Tre' continued. "Why don't you just kick him out?"

"Because Tre', he's here to see me."

"Ohhhh," Tre surmised. "That's different. Then, why aren't you sitting over there with him?"

"You sound like Onyx," Carmen fussed.

"And that's not an answer, Carmen Santiago," Tre' rebuffed.

"Tre' I don't know what to do," Carmen confided.

"That's easy," Tre' replied. "Go have dinner with the man."

Tre' didn't give Carmen time to rebut what he said. Before she knew it, Carmen was standing alone contemplating her next move. Slowly, Carmen turned around. Her eyes trailed to where Grayson sat. Turks didn't look anxious or uncomfortable. He seemed relaxed; too relaxed.

Ugggh, Carmen moaned to herself, dropping her head between her shoulders and looking up at the ceiling. Lowering her head, Carmen took a deep breath, blowing the air through her prettily painted lips. She looked in Grayson's direction, this time with intention. His eyes were right there waiting for her, as though he expected her eyes to find him. Turks watched with heightened intrigue as she moved from behind her station and took the first tentative step in his direction.

Carmen's steps were slow and calculated. She moved like a cat on the prowl; at least that's what Turks saw as he watched her every step.

"Is this seat taken," Carmen asked as she stood by his table.

"Only by you, Grayson crooned. When he saw that Carmen was committed to the idea of joining him, evidenced by the smile that dared to tease at the corner of her lips, he stood to his full height, and moved close to Carmen without touching her. Turks pulled out her chair and waited until she sat down comfortably before returning to his set.

"Glad you decided to join me," Turks smiled.

"You gave me little option, Papi," Carmen replied.

"How is that," Turks asked, leaning his elbows on the table.

"You wouldn't stop staring, haciendome incommode," Carmen sighed.

"I know," she continued. "You need a translation."

"I do," Turks replied. "Are you okay with translating for me?"

"No, I don't have a problem helping you to understand what it is I am saying," Carmen said. "Haciendome incommode means you made me uncomfortable."

"Because I appreciated how beautiful you are?"

"It sounds bad when you say it like that," Carmen sighed,

"How would you like me to say it," Turks asked. "Let me see if I can make it sound not so bad. Carmen, you are mesmerizing, alluring, breathtaking. Is that better?"

Carmen's hands went to her cheeks as though holding them would stop the color from pouring in. Grayson made her blush, which made Carmen even more uncomfortable; or maybe self-conscious is what she felt. Whatever it was, she didn't want Grayson bearing witness to her reaction firsthand. It was already bad enough that he'd been right about her joining him at the table. Weak and affected by a man's words are not how Carmen saw herself; not now anyway. She refused to let it happen with Grayson… not while he was watching.

But it was too late. Turks eyes softened as Carmen fidgeted in front of him. Yet, his desire wasn't to make her self-conscious. The night before, Turks asked Carmen to tell him something about her that no one else knew. Her reaction to his presence did just that.

Carmen eased her hands from her cheeks and rested them in her lap.

"Have you decided what you want to order?"

She needed to change the subject; to get Grayson to talk about something else.

"I have," Grayson replied going along with her diversion.

Carmen turned in her seat to gain the attention of the waitress. When she felt a warm hand on her shoulder, Carmen turned back around,

"No need for that," Turks crooned.

"I thought you decided," Carmen asked.

"I did," Turks acknowledged. "But what I want is not on the menu."

"Do I dare ask what that might be?"

"Do you," Turks inquired.

There was a moment of absolute silence between them, yet Turks eyes spoke volumes for what his lips didn't say.

"What do you want Grayson?"

Carmen could feel her heart pounding hard in her chest. There was a part of her that wanted to know the answer, and another part of her that was afraid to know; not because Grayson frightened her. That couldn't be further from the truth. She was intrigued by him; something she hadn't been in a long time… intrigued by a man.

"You, beautiful," he answered confidently. "I want you, Carmen, on the back of my bike, tonight."

Carmen's arched brows furrowed, and her eyes narrowed hearing his response. The knock of her heart remained high as it beat fervently in her chest. She watched as Grayson lifted himself from the chair and stepped out from behind the table.

"I'll see you tonight," he whispered close to her ear.

Carmen's heart skipped a beat, and her yoni thumped. Her eyes remained straightforward as Carmen leaned back in her chair.

He just won't take no for an answer…

Chapter Five

The lunch rush at Café Laquette paled in comparison to dinner service. Even after the doors opened, the line outside the café wrapped around the building.

"I don't know what Tre' and his crew are doing in that kitchen, but baby, these folks can't get enough," Onyx said as she rushed past Carmen to attend to a matter at the bar.

Carmen loved the excitement in Onyx's voice. She couldn't be happier for her. Onyx worked hard to get her restaurant up and running. Carmen was there when the banks didn't want to take a risk on a Black woman wanting to open yet another restaurant in a market the banks felt was already oversaturated. But Onyx Malone wouldn't take no for an answer. Carmen was a shoulder to lean on when Onyx felt down. But she was also there when Onyx dusted off her Christian Louboutin's and got the deal done; raising funds non-traditionally, but making it happen, nonetheless. And the success of Café Laquette made all the bankers who rejected her eat their words.

And whatever Tre' was doing in the kitchen was culinary ecstasy. It had to be. The crowds grew larger and larger as the buzz about the restaurant spread, and tonight was no exception. But Carmen loved it. She thrived in the chaos. The high level of activity in the restaurant made time fly by. That didn't give Carmen a lot of time to think or any time to fret over Grayson's imminent return.

It was midnight before the last of the customers finished their cocktails and departed the café.

"Whew chile, I am worn out," Onyx sighed, kicking off her shoes, picking them up and sitting down in the first seat she found.

"I hear you, Chica. Tonight, was insane," Carmen replied, cleaning up her station.

Onyx leaned forward in her chair. "Girl take a load off. You can do that tomorrow."

"Nah, I'm good," Carmen replied. "I'd rather come in to a clean area."

"Since when?" Tre' asked as he entered the main room. He'd overheard their conversation as he came through the door.

"Exactly," Onyx agreed. "Since when?"

Carmen stayed busy, stacking papers, and wiping down her station. She didn't give Tre' and Onyx the pleasure of a response.

"She probably still discombobulated from that man that was in here earlier," Tre' suggested, taking a seat across from Onyx.

"Hmm, that could be, Tre'," Onyx concurred.

"What do you mean discombobulado," Carmen fussed. "Tssk," Carmen hissed, dismissing Tre's commentary.

"He got you cleaning, girl," Tre' shot back. "What you call that?"

Carmen threw her hand in Tre's direction, popping her lips as she returned to the business at hand. When she heard the familiar purr of a motorcycle moving in front of the restaurant, Carmen refused to acknowledge it; outwardly that is. On the inside, she was freaking out. He actually showed up!

"Awwwww shit!" Tre' exclaimed when he saw Turks pull up in front of their spot. "Bartender! Pour me a drink! I'm ready to watch this show, honey!"

Onyx covered her mouth, trying to contain the giggle brewing on her lips. She liked the fact that Turks was persistent. That's what Carmen needed; a good man who didn't hide his interest in her. Turks didn't hide his pursuit of her. Onyx wanted to help her friend come from the shadows of her past and explore what could be out there waiting for her.

"Carmen, I'll finish that up," Onyx offered as she padded over to the maitre'd counter.

Carmen was in a flux. Onyx could tell by her scattered movements and Carmen running her fingers through her hair repeatedly. Onyx placed her hands over Carmen's, grounding her to the present.

"I can't believe he showed up," Carmen whispered. "He said he would, but I didn't believe him! "Que se supone que haga?"

"The first thing you gotta do is breath, Carmen," Onyx encouraged.

Carmen did as Onyx suggested, taking a deep breath and blowing it out slowly.

"Good, now, go to the door, open it, and step outside. Turks will take it from there."

"Why am I freaking out like this," Carmen sighed.

"Because you like him, and it's okay," Onyx replied. "Now, go. We got this."

"Uh ladies, he's at the door. Should I get it, you know, since it's late and stuff," Tre' suggested?

"Carmen's got it," Onyx interjected. "But thanks for looking out, Tre'."

"You know I have to protect my girls from all hurt, harm, and danger," Tre' chortled.

Nervously, Carmen smoothed out her slacks before walking to the door. She didn't want to look anxious by strolling too quickly, nor did she want to appear aloof by taking too long. Even so, Carmen struggled to find her natural stride as Grayson peered through the glass door. Once she arrived, Carmen unlocked the safety latched and opened the door. Grayson's ruggedly handsome face greeted Carmen and the charming smile that displayed his beautiful pearly white teeth welcomed her.

"Are you ready to ride, beautiful?"

The most Carmen could muster was a nod of the head. Grayson extended his hand to her and Carmen accepted it, feeling his firm but gentle touch for the first time. Grayson folded his hand over hers and escorted Carmen to his bike; a 2019 classic Harley Davidson Softail. It was a gorgeous bike; black on black with high-polished chrome accents. Grayson continued to hold Carmen's hand as they reached his bike. He reached to the handlebars, picking up a helmet.

"Have you ridden before?"

"No," Carmen replied.

"Do you trust me," Grayson asked. His gaze was so deep and penetrating, Carmen felt like Grayson was looking through her. She also felt like Grayson could read her honest thoughts without Carmen saying a word.

"I don't know what to say, Grayson," Carmen admitted, looking away.

Carefully, Grayson lifted his hand, placing his finger under Carmen's chin. Slowly he lifted her head, so Carmen's eyes met his. Even then, it took Carmen a moment to return Grayson's steady gaze.

"Say what you mean, beautiful," Grayson reassured.

"I'll ride with you, Grayson, but it's going to take some time for me to trust you."

"That I understand," Grayson answered.

"With no translation," Carmen smiled.

"With no translation."

Grayson lifted the helmet to Carmen. She received it with both hands and placed it on her head.

"Let me help you with that," Grayson offered. She nodded her permission, and he reached over, adjusting the helmet and locking the chin strap.

"Is that comfortable?"

"Yes," Carmen replied, smoothing down her hair as she spoke.

Grayson turned slightly from her and mounted his bike. Turning the key in the ignition, the Harley roared to life. Grayson reached out an upturned hand to Carmen. Taking a step forward, she folded her hand in his and moved closer to the bike.

"I've got you," Grayson said. Only this time Carmen heard the smooth of Grayson's voice like he was inside her head. Carmen looked surprised and then she smiled realizing the helmet was miked. Lifting her leg, Carmen mounted the bike and for the first time, felt the power of the roaring engine between her thighs.

"Whew," she squealed in response.

"You'll get used to it," Grayson suggested as he secured his helmet.

"That's if I ride again," Carmen quipped.

"You will."

Grayson revved the engine and lifted the kickstand.

"Grayson, you'll start off slow, right? Carmen asked.

"Of course, beautiful. I want you to want to ride with me again," Grayson smiled. "It's easier if you hold on to me."

"You would like that, wouldn't you," Carmen sassed.

"Maybe," Grayson smirked.

Carmen leaned in, placing her hands against his firm waist. Grayson folded his lips in and slowly released them. He liked the way Carmen's hands felt against his form. Grayson did as he said he would, taking it easy at a slow rate of speed down the neighborhood street. He could feel Carmen relax as her hands moved further around his torso and he felt the softness of her body resting against him.

"Are you ready to go faster," Grayson inquired.

"No lo se, Papi, I don't know," Carmen smiled. Grayson could hear the lightness of her tone and feel the smile he heard in Carmen's voice. Grayson smiled. He loved when Carmen called him Papi. When Grayson felt Carmen's arms tighten around his waist, he knew her answer.

"Si, Papi, let's go faster," Carmen giggled. "Just a little."

Grayson ran his thick hand across hers as he turned the bike toward the interstate. Carmen started to get excited.

"Don't laugh at me if I start to scream, si?"

"I make no promises," Grayson laughed.

"Papi," Carmen pleaded as Grayson steered onto the on-ramp. The bike started to pick up speed, as the engine powerfully roared beneath them. Carmen wasn't afraid, which surprised her. At some level, she accepted that she trusted Grayson, to a certain degree, or she'd never climbed on the bike in the first place.

Consider the possibilities…

Grayson leveled the speed of the bike at sixty miles an hour; fast enough to feel but not so fast that it scared Carmen. Carmen heard Onyx's voice in her head as the speed of the bike increased. Carmen felt her hair lift from her shoulder and the wind caressing her face. Carmen also felt the strength of Turks pressed against her. All of it felt good, really good.

"Wooo!" Carmen exclaimed as she lifted her hands overhead and let the wind rush over here. "Esto es increible!"

"Translation," Grayson smiled.

"This is amazing, Papi! Esto es increible!"

Carmen laced her arms around Grayson's waist and squeezed him tight. The smile she wore was hard to erase.

Grayson slowed the bike and exited the interstate. Carmen recognized where he pulled the Harley over. Grayson parked the motorcycle and lowered the kickstand, after turning off the ignition. He helped Carmen off the bike and then got off the bike himself.

"Helmet please," Grayson asked.

Carmen obliged, removing her helmet and handing it to Grayson. Carmen ran her fingers through her hair.

"Please tell me I don't have helmet hair," Carmen began.

"No, your hair is beautiful as always," Grayson replied. "Walk with me?"

"Sure," Carmen replied.

Centennial Park in downtown Atlanta was known for rhythmically dancing waterfalls, live bands, and green space. In 2000, the park was the site of the Summer Olympic Games torch lighting ceremony. The park was nostalgic as much as it was interactive. And tonight? There was a hint of romance in the air. Grayson and Carmen walked side by side around the circular fountain. Grayson was mindful to shorten his stride, so Carmen could keep a comfortable pace. Although the breeze in the park was nothing like it was when Carmen was on the back of the Harley, it was still nice

"Why do they call you Turks," Carmen asked as they found a seat beside the fountain.

"Because of where I'm from, Turks and Cacaos," Grayson replied.

"That's an island, right?"

"Yes, it is," Grayson replied.

"You gave up island life for traffic congestion, temperamental weather, and crowds, why?"

"The same reason most people come to Atlanta, the Black Mecca, you know? There were greater opportunities here for the kind of work that I do."

"And what is that," Carmen asked.

"I'm an architect."

"Really?" The not so subtle surprise in Carmen's voice was not lost on Grayson.

"Oh, I see," Grayson crooned. "You thought all I did was ride."

"No," Carmen defended. "I figured you did something."

"Say mechanic or assistant manager at a gas station," Grayson taunted.

Carmen lifted her shoulders and feigned a smile.

"That is what you thought, isn't it beautiful?"

"Revantado," Carmen replied. "I am so busted!"

Grayson reached for her; grabbing Carmen playfully around the waist and pulling her to him. The sound of her laughter tickled his ears and reminded Grayson why he was drawn to Carmen in the first place.

"Ah, Papi, don't make me laugh!"

Grayson chuckled. "I like it when you call me Papi."

"I bet you do," Carmen smiled.

She didn't mind that Grayson didn't move his hand as they continued to talk.

"Tell me why no man has swept you off your feet yet," Grayson asked. He wanted to get to know Carmen; to know everything about her.

"I'm heavy," Carmen replied, turning her face toward the dancing waters of the fountain. Grayson heard the realness of her response; the honesty of what she said and didn't say. He turned and examined her profile as Carmen looked off into the distance. His eyes searched her face, reaching into her thoughts. The focus in her eyes was absent. Grayson felt the need to be quiet; to let Carmen tell him what she meant what she wanted him to know. Grayson was willing to wait as long as it took. Even if she didn't say it now, Grayson was still willing to wait.

"I'm heavy because I have baggage; packages I carry with me that I can't seem to let go. At times, I put those bags down because they feel too heavy to carry or I get tired from the extra weight."

Grayson could see Carmen's shoulders slowly drop as though the weight she described was bearing down on her right then.

"But somehow," Carmen smiled insincerely, "I manage to pick them up again, no matter how many times I tell myself that I don't want to carry them anymore. That's why I'm single, Papi. I've got baggage."

"Have you ever considered, beautiful, that there's someone willing to carry your bags for you?"

Grayson's question caught Carmen off guard. She never considered that such a thing was possible; that someone like that even existed.

"Why would someone do that?" Carmen's eyes were drawn back to Grayson

The innocent sincerity of Carmen's question pricked Grayson's heart.

"Because, you're too special to carry that weight alone."

Tenderly, Carmen's eyes melted into his dark pools. They were drawn to each other like a magnetic force neither of them controlled. Carmen could feel the sincerity of his words reflected in Grayson's eyes. Something intense rose through their mutual entrancement. Carmen felt powerless to resist the pull she felt from Grayson; her own internal push to eradicate the space of distance between them. Grayson's lips slowly descended to meet hers. Carmen drank in the sweetness of his mouth as Grayson's persuasive lips caressed hers. His was a kiss for Carmen's tired soul to melt into. And when their lips parted, and Grayson remained close, it was just as sweet.

For some reason, the ride home felt even freer for Carmen. She fully rested, leaning fully into the strength of Grayson's back. She was comfortable enough to allow Grayson to take her home. Onyx trusted Grayson. He was good friends with Egypt. Those two factors helped bridge the gap in Carmen's own assessment. When they arrived, Grayson parked his bike in front of Carmen's house and then walked her to the door. Carmen felt her heart beating faster in her chest after being so calm just moments before. Carmen wiggled her fingers trying to keep the adrenaline coursing through her veins from spilling over.

"I had a nice time, Grayson. Thank you."

"I guess nice is good," Grayson replied.

"Nice is good, Papi."

Carmen was even more nervous as they reached her front door. Most men who walked Carmen to the front door expected to go inside. Carmen hoped she was wrong about Grayson.

"So, since it was nice, does that mean you'll ride with me again?"

"Yes, Grayson, I would ride with you again."

"That, beautiful, is music to my ears. I had a nice time as well."

Grayson could see the slight shift in Carmen's disposition. Although he would love to recreate the kiss at the fountain. Grayson reined in his desire. Grayson respected Carmen and by extension, the nonverbal boundaries she set. Besides, he wasn't looking for a one-night stand. Grayson wanted something more with Carmen.

"I don't want this moment to be awkward between us," Grayson began. "So, I'm going to kiss you on the forehead, and then I'm going to step back and wait until you are safely inside your apartment," Grayson announced. "Is that okay with you?"

Carmen smiled. Although some would have considered Grayson taking the time to explain his next actions were weak, Carmen didn't see it that way. His expression was one of the manliest things she'd heard in a long time.

"That is good with me, Papi."

Grayson smiled and then leaned in. Carmen closed her eyes in anticipation of the kiss. When his lips touched her flesh, it was as tender, gentle, and unexpected in a knowing way. Carmen lingered there, in the purity of that moment. Grayson did just what he said. After he kissed her, he stepped back and waited until she took her keys from her purse and unlocked the door.

"Good night, beautiful."

"Good night, Grayson."

Carmen was still smiling when she closed the door.

Chapter Six

When Onyx arrived at the café the next morning, Carmen was already there. Onyx stood back and watched as Carmen flounced around, attending to her work station, warmly greeting the other staff, and sashaying her voluptuous hips more than usual. Onyx saw Tre' entering the kitchen. She quietly got his attention and called him over. Onyx didn't have to say anything. All she had to do was point in Carmen's direction, and Tre' got the picture. Tre' had to cover his mouth to keep Carmen from hearing his guffaw.

"Wait just one minute," Onyx gasped, dramatically covering her heart with her hand. "If I had pearls, trust me, I would be clutching them."

"You and me too," Tre' added.

Carmen heard their conversation but didn't give them the satisfaction of turning around and responding. She was in too good a mood. Carmen refused to allow their petty antics to ruin her mood. But Onyx and Tre' refused to be ignored. They approached Carmen from behind and stood with their arms crossing their chests and Onyx obnoxiously patting her foot demanding that Carmen turn around. When she continued to ignore them, Onyx cleared her throat and Tre' repeatedly tapped Carmen on the shoulder until she was so irritated, Carmen spun on her heels to face them.

"Good morning Onyx, Good morning Tre'," Carmen sang with a broad smile.

Onyx's eyes narrowed and Tre's furrowed.

"Mornin'," they chorused flatly.

"Tre', I have an observation, not a complaint but an observation," Onyx began.

"Go ahead with your observation, boss lady," Tre' sighed.

"Our dear Carmen is never early for work, never, but that's more of a curiosity than anything."

"I'm with you so far," Tre' replied.

"So, here's the observation. Yesterday, less than 24 hours ago, our dear sweet Carmen's disposition was sullen, melancholy, low even." Onyx continued. "But today, she is like a ball of sunshine; humming, dancing lightly on her feet. Her entire disposition has changed. Now, I wonder why that is?"

"No disrespect, boss, but I think you're asking the wrong question," Tre' suggested. Tre' disregarded the smirk that turned the corners of Carmen's lips and the periodic eye roll she shot between him and Onyx.

"Well Tre', what is the right question?"

"Not why that is but who that is," Tre' answered.

"Aha," Onyx gasped.

They both turned their full attention to Carmen for a response. They got one as Carmen's cheeks filled with color and the dagger stare, she'd been given could no longer be maintained.

"Why can't you just say good morning, lo dices en serio, I mean, really?" Carmen countered. "And most bosses would be thrilled when their employees arrived early, not questioning it."

"You're right, Carmen," Onyx replied. "I like to see you arrive early. Even if it never happens again, I will remember this day."

"But you are missing the most important question," Tre' interjected.

"Which is," Carmen asked, although she knew precisely what Tre' referred to.

"Girl, how did the date go??" Tre' demanded and Onyx seconded.

"It was nice," Carmen smiled.

"It was nice," Onyx smiled. It wasn't the words Carmen said, it was how she said them, and the ones she kept to herself.

"Nice?? Chile, I need the details," Tre' scoffed. "I don't have time for the shenanigans," Tre' fussed walking away from the ladies.

"So, are you okay, Carmen? I mean really," Onyx asked. "I know you had reservations about Turks, but it turned out okay?"

"I'm good, surprisingly," Carmen admitted.

"Squee," Onyx yelped, throwing her arms around Carmen's neck and pulling her in tight. "This makes me very happy," Onyx smiled.

"It was just one date, Chica," Carmen giggled.

"I know," Onyx replied, as she stepped back from Carmen and placed her hands on Carmen's shoulders and looking her straight in the eye. "But you let Turks in, even if it was just a little bit. That's huge Carmen."

Carmen nodded her head and smiled. She knew Onyx's words were heartfelt and Onyx only wanted the best for her.

"Would it be too forward if I asked when you'll be seeing him again?"

"I have no idea," Carmen laughed. "We didn't even exchange phone numbers!"

Carmen didn't have to wait long, and it didn't matter that Turks didn't have her phone number. He showed up at the close of business like he had the night before and took Carmen on another high energy romantic ride. His approach was just as unassumingly sexy and just as personable and caring. Carmen started to believe that it wasn't a fluke; that the Grayson she got to know the night before was real not fantasy.

"So where are you whisking me off to tonight, Papi," Carmen asked through the miked helmet.

"You'll see soon enough, beautiful," Grayson replied.

Carmen was good with his response. She relaxed against Grayson with her arms laced tightly around his waist and enjoyed the ride. Grayson leaned back into her and stroked her hands as they rode, with the smooth sounds of Anthony Hamilton providing melodic, rhythmic sounds to their ride. When Grayson pulled onto a gravelly road with little light, Carmen held on just a little tighter. Grayson turned down the music.

"We're almost there."

"Where is there," Carmen giggled.

Grayson slowed the bike underneath them as the gravelly road became smooth. Grayson pulled the bike up a slope that required Carmen to hold on even tighter. As the bike evened out, Grayson stopped it, putting the bike in park and turning off the ignition. Grayson helped Carmen off the bike, took her helmet and lifted his frame from the bike as well.

"Take my hand beautiful," Grayson said, after taking off his helmet and placing it on the bike. Carmen did as Grayson requested. He reached into his pocket, pulling out a penlight and illuminated the area in front of them.

"Be careful, Grayson replied. He tucked Carmen's arm under his while maintaining contact with her hand and led Carmen down the lit path. There was an air of intrigue and excitement as they traversed down the road. When Grayson stopped and lifted the light to a door, Carmen stopped with him.

"There's something I want to show you."

Releasing Carmen's hand for just a moment, Grayson input a code into a lock on the door and opened it. He reached inside, and flicked a switch, illuminating a hallway.

"Ready?"

"Yes," Carmen replied even though she was unsure what that something was.

Grayson turned off the penlight and returned it to his pocket. Wrapping his thickly muscled arm around Carmen's waist, he escorted her down the hallway. At the end of that space, Grayson reached around another wall and hit a series of switches that illuminated the entirety of the space. The two walked into the space and Grayson watched as Carmen looked around.

"What is this place," Carmen mused as her eyes traveled from the height of the ceilings down to the hardwood floors.

"A new home I designed," Grayson began, "my home."

Seriously, Papi? This is amazing," Carmen replied. "I want to see everything!"

There was no greater compliment that could be paid to a man like Grayson. He found it hard to hide the smile that emerged on his face behind Carmen's excitement and interest.

"Come on, show me," Carmen encouraged as she reached for Grayson's hand. He gladly folded his hand in hers and escorted Carmen on the grand sure; highlighting the architectural details and style choices from the exotic Brazilian Tiger-wood hardwood floors to the steel and glass chandeliers that darted the ceilings. But that's not all Carmen saw. She noticed the intricate detailing of the staircase and the crease-free windows that spanned the distance of the walls in the rear of the home.

"And this is my office, Grayson announced as they entered another space.

"So, this is where the magic happens," Carmen said as she roamed through the space. She traced her hand along the edge of Grayson's desk and eyed his shelves, replete with rows and rows of books. Grayson leaned on the door frame and watched her as she moved. When she turned to face him, wearing an impeccable smile, he felt his heart start to melt.

"How does it start," Carmen asked as she traipsed in Grayson's direction. it was something about Carmen's walk that instantly turned Grayson on. His eyes moved from the crown of her head down to her feet and then deliberately back again, stopping at her entrancing eyes.

"How does what start," Grayson crooned as Carmen stopped short right in front of him.

"The creative process," Carmen asked. "The process that leads to something as incredible as this."

Grayson was flattered. His eyes simmered, and his lips were slightly upturned in a smile. "We can talk about that over a glass of wine. Are you good with that?"

"You have wine here," Carmen asked.

"Yes," Grayson replied, reaching out to Carmen and extending his hand. She willingly accepted. "Even though I haven't officially moved in I like to come here and work some-times. It's secluded, quiet…"

"I get that," Carmen smiled.

The duo traveled down the spiral staircase into the kitchen. "You designed this kitchen like you're a chef,"

Carmen observed. "Is that you, Papi? Chef Grayson? Were you just frontin' at the lesson with Onyx and Egypt?"

Grayson laughed. "No, beloved, I wasn't frontin'," Grayson explained. "I do okay; an omelet here or there. But, I'm a beast on the grill."

"So why such an amazing kitchen," Carmen inquired, leaning against the counter and maintaining her focus on Grayson.

"Just in case," Grayson began, popping the cork on the wine bottle.

Carmen's raised brow suggested she needed more than that.

"Just in case the woman who steals my heart wants a state-of-the-art kitchen with all the bells and whistles."

"Even if she can't cook?" Carmen smiled.

"Even if she can't cook worth a damn," Grayson chortled. "Like me."

"Good to know," Carmen purred. Grayson seductively winked his eye as he folded in his bottom lip releasing it slowly.

"Would you mind grabbing the wine glasses from that cabinet next to you?"

"Not at all, Carmen answered. Pivoting on her three-inch heels, Carmen reached for the high polished silver knob. The wine glasses were hidden behind frosted glass but illuminated by under cabinet lighting that gave the objects in the cabinet a warm silhouetted glow. Even with her stilettoes on, Carmen had to tiptoe to reach the bottom level shelf. Grayson thought it was cute, but he made a mental note about cabinet height adjustment, just in case. After closing the cabinet, Carmen padded to the kitchen sink and rinsed the glasses. She used the towel balanced on the sink to dry them.

"Let's go this way, beautiful," Grayson said as Carmen finished up.

Carmen wasn't sure where they were headed. She thought

she had seen the entire house. But she hadn't. There was another hallway behind the kitchen. She heard something that sounded familiar, but Carmen couldn't place the sound. When Grayson turned on the light, Carmen realized what she heard. It was water.

"Oh, Papi, this is amazing," Carmen sighed as the indoor pool came into view. The sound of the water was soothing, and the dark green leafed plants that accentuated the corners of the pool provided added visual interest. The wall opposite the pool was entirely glass; offering a seamless view of the landscape beyond.

"And if you look really close, you can see my bar-be-cue grill right there," Grayson said as the two gazed out of the window.

"You were serious about grilling, huh," Carmen laughed.

"Absolutely," Grayson replied with a smile. He turned and placed the wine bottle on a nearby table and retrieved the glasses from Carmen.

"Will you sit with me," Grayson asked, pointing towards the pool. Carmen looked up at him and then down at the pool.

"Sure," Carmen smiled.

"Cool," Grayson smiled. He walked a few steps away retrieving cushioned pillows that he placed near the edge of the pool. Grayson returned to Carmen.

"Let me help you with your shoes," Grayson suggested. Carmen smiled as Grayson bent his tall frame down beside her.

"You can lean on me," he suggested as Carmen lifted one foot for Grayson to remove one of her shoes and then the other. Grayson cuffed the bottom of Carmen's slacks high enough to not get wet. Even with that, Grayson was gentle with Carmen, attentive to her. His actions didn't go unnoticed. Carmen did lean on his strength to keep her balance, feeling the ripples of his muscled back beneath her fingertips.

Grayson paired Carmen's shoes up and sat them by the wall. Then he removed his shoes and set them to the side. Once he was seated on the cushion, Grayson helped Carmen to sit down next to him. After she was comfortably settled, Grayson poured the wine and extended a glass to Carmen.

Carmen barely extended her toe to test the water.

"Go ahead, it's warm," Grayson encouraged. Carmen looked back at Grayson before testing the water again.

"Oh wow," Carmen sighed, "Hace calor. It is warm."

"Told you," Grayson said, extending his glass for a toast. Carmen acquiesced, taking a sip of the sweet wine herself.

"Isn't there something you're supposed to be telling me," Carmen asked.

"How it all starts, right?"

"Yes," Carmen asked, genuinely curious. "Tengo muchas ganas de saber."

Grayson's eyebrow raised.

"I really want to know," Carmen explained.

Grayson didn't intend to belabor the point. It's just that the women he'd dated in the past were much more interested in his bank account than what contributed to the account. Having someone genuinely curious about his art, genuinely interested in his process, did something unexpected to Grayson's heart. He was fortunate in that his passion paid the bills and afforded him a comfortable lifestyle. Yet, he hadn't managed to find the one to share his everything with. He was flattered, and although Carmen raised the question, Grayson was even more intrigued than ever.

"Can I be honest with you," Grayson began.

"Of course, Papi," Carmen replied. "Why be anything else?"

Grayson nodded and covered a smile that tread across his lips. The smile was an unconscious reaction to what he wanted to say; that he otherwise would have been too embarrassed to say. He would have to trust Carmen in this moment.

Grayson paused for a moment, taking another drink of the wine before he began.

"We were pretty poor growing up. My mom and dad did the best they could while he was alive, but after he passed away, things got pretty bad for mom, my younger brother and myself. We lived in an apartment until my mom couldn't keep up with the payments. She worked two jobs, busted her ass, but it still wasn't enough to pay all the bills and take care of us. So, at one point, we ended up going to a shelter. It's funny you know. Shelters are supposed to be there to help people who are having a hard time, to prevent people from being homeless, you know? But there are so many rules and restrictions that the people the shelters are supposed to help aren't getting the help they need."

Grayson paused, reflectively swirling the dark liquid in his wine glass. Carmen could hear panged emotion, both sadness, and anger in Grayson's voice as she listened.

"In order to get a spot, we had to get to the shelter early in the morning, like when the sun came up; standing in line and hope by the time we reached the front, that there would still be space available. Standing in line those mornings, trying to find a spot, people pushing and shoving; not because they were mean but because they were frustrated and desperate, my brother and I missed school. Miss too much school, the school refers to you as truant. The social worker is dispatched to determine the reason. A petition is filed with the courts holding your parent responsible for your absence. Yet, you don't want to tell people the reason you were absent is that you had to try to find a bed to sleep in. That kind of information makes the situation for your parent worse because now they are considered neglectful, not just poor."

Although Carmen's childhood had not been so dire, she could certainly empathize with Grayson's situation. She could feel his hurt and his pain as he spoke.

"If there wasn't space, we had few options; try to hole up

with family that was few and far between, or sleep in the car. But we lucked out," Grayson feigned a smile, "and for a week or so, we had a spot at the shelter. We had to leave by seven o'clock every morning and had to get back to the shelter by six, or we would be locked out. Can you imagine all those moms and all those kids trying to get ready? A few showers, no real privacy, no real place to keep your belongings. You had to hide your stuff, so people wouldn't steal what little you had. But they were thieves out of desperation, lack of opportunity."

There was a deep, weighty sigh that passed between Grayson's lips as he looked out over the water. His gaze was steady, yet Carmen could tell, even from where she was sitting, that his eyes were unfocused staring at nothing.

"Rows of bunk beds lined the one big room we were in. Although the sheets were clean, they were stained, probably from the last person who slept there, or maybe even the person before that. The mattresses were flat against hard steel frames like the beds you imagine in a jail cell," Grayson chuckled from the memory.

"They were hard as hell! But we were grateful for those beds. It was better than the alternative. The shelter we were in didn't allow men, so it was moms and their children. It was loud and sometimes crazy. People were tired and worn down from the struggle, you know? The one thing that I liked to do was draw. I guess you could call it my happy place."

Grayson's face lit up when he talked about it. For the first time since he started talking about the situation, Grayson turned in Carmen's direction.

"There was a television in the shelter, but I didn't want to fight with anybody to watch it. They had some play areas set up for the kids. They were kind of sparse, a few toys here and there. But what they did have was some construction paper, crayons and broken pencils. That's all I needed. Before the shelter, my drawings were aimless, random. But after spending a few nights in that place, my drawings became my dreams on paper. I drew the house my mother deserved. I showed it to her, my mom. And to see her eyes well with tears at my rudimentary artwork, touched me. She saw the intentions of my heart. She saw my dream for her."

Carmen had to choke back her own emotions hearing the depth of feelings Grayson shared. She could tell how much Grayson loved his mother as his eyes momentarily misted over describing the same for her. This was the reason; the reason Grayson became an architect. Carmen reached out to Grayson, extending an upturned hand. She wanted to connect with him, to let Grayson know she was there with him. Grayson's eyes lowered, seeing Carmen's outstretched hand. He willingly folded his hand into hers and appreciated the warmth of her touch as Carmen interlaced her fingers with his.

"We weren't able to stay at the shelter long. Two preteen boys were frowned upon in a place like that. I didn't realize that my mom had to lie to get us in. but she was our mom. She did what she had to do to protect us. Somebody found out though, and they wouldn't let us stay. They told my mom she could stay and that they would find beds for us at the men's shelter, but mom didn't want us separated. She wanted us to stay together as a family, and so that's what we did. We ended up sleeping in the car, but we were together. My mom taped that picture of the house I drew to the inside front window of our car. I would see her looking at that picture. Sometimes she would smile. Sometimes, she would cry. I think it was at that moment that I decided that no matter what I had to do, I was going to give my mom the house she deserved…"

"And you did, didn't you," Carmen asked.

"Yeah, I did."

"Your mother must be so proud of you," Carmen sighed as their hands remained connected.

"She is," Grayson replied." Always has been, even when I was drawing stick figures.

"That is such a sweet story," Carmen continued. "Thanks for sharing it with me."

"You're the first one," Grayson admitted.

"Seriamente? Seriously?"

"Yes, seriamente," Grayson answered. The look in his eyes spoke volumes even before he uttered the words. "I trusted you enough to tell you."

Carmen felt that. She trusted him, too; more than she felt she should have in the time she'd known Grayson. But what Carmen felt was real. Her heart told her so. Carmen rested her head on Grayson's strong shoulder as they sat quietly enjoying the peace and serenity the water offered. There was something between them. They both felt it. Whether it was an escalating heartbeat or that weird, unsettled feeling, they both had in the pits of their stomachs, that something was there. And Grayson refused to let that moment get away from him. He turned inward bringing his face to Carmen and his mouth to hers. Carmen closed her eyes as their lips connected. Grayson's kiss was firm; given with intention. She succumbed to his probing tongue relishing in the way Grayson made her feel. Sitting the wine glass down, Carmen raised her hand, cupping the back of Grayson's head, keeping him there with her as they willingly explored. The temperature in the room seemed to increase ten-fold as Grayson wrapped his arms around Carmen's waist; devouring her mouth with his. There was a dreamy intimacy in their kiss, more than either of them ever imagined.

And when they separated, on a soft sweet kiss, the intimacy remained.

Chapter Seven

And for the next three weeks, the bond between Carmen and Grayson grew. They spent all their free time together, getting to know each other, enjoying each other's company. And when they weren't physically together, Grayson and Carmen spent endless hours on the telephone, laughing and talking about everything; from local politics to the weather to their personal goals and dreams. The conversation never got old. Carmen never grew tired of hearing the sexy of his baritone, throaty, sensual voice. It did get to be old hat though, in the most pleasant way; Grayson coming every night to pick Carmen up from work on his Harley; the two of them riding off into the proverbial sunset no matter what time of day it was.

One evening, Turks pulled into the Mercedes Benz Stadium parking lot.

"What are we doing here," Carmen asked as Turks planted his feet on the ground and turned off the bike.

"I want to cruise with you," Grayson crooned.

"We've been doing that," Carmen replied smilingly.

"Not with you driving," Grayson smiled.

Carmen's brow lifted as what Grayson suggested started to register. "Quieres que conduzca?"

"If that means I want you to drive, then yes," Grayson laughed.

"Oh, Dios mio," Carmen sighed, wringing her hands together.

"You'll be fine," Grayson crooned. "I'll be right there with you."

"Promesa? Promise," Carmen asked.

"You already know," Grayson reassured. After stepping off the bike and balancing it, he asked Carmen to move to the front. She was reluctant but did as Grayson asked. She felt better as Grayson positioned himself behind her, taking most of the weight of the bike onto his strong legs.

"Okay, I want you to start the bike, and then I'll lift the kickstand once we get started."

Carmen looked back over her shoulder, seeing if Grayson was serious. His smile indicated that he definitely was. There was some apprehension as Carmen turned the key in the ignition. Yet, as soon as she felt the hum of the bike underneath her, Carmen started to get excited. After lifting the kickstand, Grayson leaned forward, balancing his hands on the handlebar alongside Carmen's.

"Ready, beautiful?"

Carmen lifted her hand temporarily from the bar and completed the sign of the cross over herself.

"Si, Papi, I'm ready."

She started off slowly, getting a feel for how to move the bike. Grayson was right there as he promised, giving her instructions through the mic. His voice was soothing and supportive as Carmen started to navigate the bike around the empty lot.

"I think I'm getting the hang of it," Carmen squealed as she gained confidence in her ability.

"You're doing fantastic, babe," Grayson encouraged.

Grayson smiled as he watched Carmen getting more comfortable. She barely noticed when he removed one hand and then the other from the handlebars.

"Weee," Carmen exclaimed as she sped up, feeling the wind move against her helmet.

That was the first time Grayson let Carmen drive the Harley, but it wasn't the last.

It was near the end of another crazily busy Sunday afternoon brunch, and Carmen was rushing to finish up fully anticipating that Turks would be arriving shortly. Once her station was straightened, Carmen sashayed off to the ladies' room to freshen up. Although Grayson always told Carmen how beautiful she was, Carmen didn't want to disappoint. There was a smile that teetered on the corners of her lips. The past three weeks had been a welcome reprieve for Carmen. She relaxed and actually had something, someone to look forward to. Carmen ran her fingers through her tresses and checked her lip gloss for just the right shine. When she exited the ladies' room, a waitress coming from the opposite direction got Carmen's attention.

"There's someone up front to see you."

Carmen smiled and did a little shoulder shimmy. She knew who that someone was, and she couldn't wait to see him again. The sashay in Carmen's hips increased as Carmen made her way to the main room. Naturally, Carmen looked outside for Grayson's bike.

"Mi señora."

Carmen's feet stopped short. That voice; she knew it all too well. Carmen's eyes closed as her heart sank. When she heard the sound of his steel toed boots slowly moving in her direction, Carmen's head dropped, and so did her shoulders. She wasn't walking as tall anymore.

"Mi señora, se que me escuchas," he uttered as footfalls brought him closer.

"Yes, I heard you," Carmen mumbled, refusing to raise

her head. She didn't want to see him. She didn't want to look at him. She didn't want him to be there. But he was… Juan Carlos.

"Baby, you look beautiful," he moaned as he grabbed Carmen around the waist and pulled her into him. Her head flopped from the abruptness of his grab. Her hands instantly went up to shield her from the hug Juan Carlos insisted on giving her. Carmen pressed hard against his chest, not wanting to be enveloped by him. But he was stronger. Juan Carlos had always been stronger.

"How did you find me," Carmen hissed as her nose was assaulted by the cologne Juan Carlos wore. It was the same scent she found so enticing when she was younger.

"That's easy," Juan Carlos grunted. "Siempre se donde estas, señora. I always know where you are. But I expected you to be there when I got out," he moaned against Carmen's ear; his warm breath stinging her sensibilities.

"I was working," Carmen insisted; still trying to detach herself from Juan Carlos' clutches.

"I'm not mad, no esto loco, mi amour," Juan Carlos groaned as he held on to Carmen. "We're together now."

Carmen felt sick to her stomach. She felt even sicker when she heard the familiar sound of Grayson's Harley pulling up to the restaurant. How would she explain Juan Carlos? Trying to pry herself from his clutches was useless.

"Aren't you off work," Juan Carlos asked as he finally released Carmen, just long enough to grab her by the hand and fold it into his curved arm. Carmen looked around, trying to find Onyx, Tre' or somebody who could intervene with Grayson on her behalf. She didn't want Grayson to see her like this.

"I still have things to do before I go," Carmen said defensively.

"Where's your friend girl who runs this place," Juan Carlos asked looking around. "I'm sure you told her I was coming home. We need to celebrate. She'll let you get off for that," Juan Carlos insisted. Now he was looking for Onyx as hard as Carmen was. Carmen's eyes were drawn to the front of the café. There Grayson was getting off his bike. He wasn't facing the restaurant. Carmen wasn't sure whether that was a good or bad thing. She needed to find Onyx. She would know what to do.

"Excuse me." Juan Carlos tapped one of the servers on the shoulder. "Where's your boss?"

The server's eyes traveled from Juan to Carmen and back to Juan Carlos again, unsure of what his reply should be. When the server looked back at Carmen again, she nodded her head and smiled as though giving the server permission to answer honestly.

"I'll get her for you," the server replied. "Who should I say is asking for her?"

"Juan Carlos."

The server walked off in search of the owner. Carmen didn't know what to do. If she approached Grayson while Juan Carlos was around, Juan would undoubtedly make a scene, embarrassing her, embarrassing himself. At the same time, she didn't want Grayson to see her with Juan especially the way Juan Carlos was holding on to her like they meant something to each other. She chastised herself as she stood there unsure what to do. Had she been forthright with Juan Carlos and told him she moved on, maybe she wouldn't be in this situation. Yet, Carmen wasn't even sure that would work. Not with Juan. He wasn't used to not getting what he wanted. He certainly wouldn't expect rejection from Carmen. Her heart beat erratically in her chest. Carmen could feel a full-on panic attack brewing. But she couldn't let Juan see her nervously anxious. He would want to know why. He would ask questions Carmen didn't know how to answer, and even if she did Juan Carlos wouldn't like the answers to.

Carmen's heart skipped a beat when she saw Grayson moving

towards the door. It was like things were moving in slow motion. Or, maybe that's just the way Carmen was processing them, slowly so she could try to figure out what the hell to do. It was getting harder though, to keep her emotions in check. Carmen tried to ease her hand from Juan Carlo's hold. Carmen could feel her hands getting clammy and starting to sweat. Her eyes moved between the two men when Juan Carlos wasn't paying attention. Instead of letting Carmen go, Juan Carlos tucked Carmen's hand in even tighter as Onyx rounded the corner.

Hearing that Carmen's criminal ex requested her, tipped Onyx off to the potential calamity in the front of her restaurant. She didn't want to rush in and be presumptuous, but Onyx couldn't imagine that Juan being at Café Laquette at closing time was a good thing. When she saw Carmen's face, Onyx knew her first instinct was right. This was not a good thing.

"Juan Carlos? I'm the proprietor of the café. Is there something I can help you with?"

Onyx was speaking to Juan Carlos, but her eyes were on Carmen. They had been friends long enough for Onyx to feel Carmen's energy, to read her nonverbals. When Carmen's eyes darted to the door and widened unnaturally, Onyx knew she had to intervene in a big way and fast.

"Yeah," Juan Carlos gruffed. "Me and my girl have some celebrating to do. I was wondering if she could cut out early so we can get started? I figured I would ask you, since you're the boss."

"Give me just one minute," Onyx said with a smile as she backed away, not giving Juan Carlos a chance to respond. Spinning on her heels, Onyx made her way over to Grayson. He greeted Onyx with a smile, but his attention was elsewhere. The smile quickly faded.

"Walk with me," Onyx encouraged, taking Turks by the arm.

Grayson looked in Carmen's direction once more and read her lips as she said, 'I'm sorry' without making a sound. His eyes stayed trained on Carmen until he felt the urging of Onyx's touch. Onyx didn't stop walking until she and Turks were outside.

"I know this whole thing is weird and I don't have a whole lot of time to explain, but please don't hold this against Carmen. This guy showing up was completely unexpected, and she is ashamed and embarrassed, and as soon as she gets a chance, she'll explain everything. I promise," Onyx said. The words flew fast from her lips and Grayson noted the urgency in her eyes.

"Is she okay?"

"She will be," Onyx said, trying to be reassuring. "I'm not going to let her leave with that guy."

"He's no stranger though" Grayson observed.

"No, he's not," Onyx admitted. "He's a regrettable part of Carmen's history."

"Should I stick around, just in case things don't go to plan?"

"I hope it doesn't come to that," Onyx sighed. "But maybe you and Egypt should stay close?"

"Done," Turks replied. "Take care of my girl," Grayson said.

"Done."

Turks mounted his bike and turned the key, bringing the Harley to life. Any other time, hearing the sound of Grayson's bike would be music to Carmen's ears. But this time, it represented Grayson leaving without her. There was a profound sadness there. Carmen didn't know if she would ever see Grayson again. But her thoughts couldn't linger with the one that was leaving. Carmen had to figure out what to do about the one that remained. She watched Onyx reenter the restaurant and Carmen tried to read Onyx's face to give her some indication of how Grayson reacted. But Onyx had already refocused her attention on Juan Carlos.

"I'm sorry about that," Onyx said. "You were saying something about Carmen getting off early?"

"Yeah," Juan Carlos replied. "We need to make up for lost time, you know?"

"I'm not sure that I do," Onyx replied offering a polite smile. "Unfortunately, I can't let Carmen leave right now."

Carmen didn't intend to sigh as loudly as she did, but it passed through her lips before she could stop it. Maybe Carmen's response was premature though as evidenced by the possessive hand that grabbed Carmen around the waist while Juan Carlos still held on tight to her other hand.

"Are you sure about that," Juan Carlos challenged. The bass in Juan's voice deepened. He didn't like to be told no. Onyx was telling him no.

"I am absolutely certain, sir," Onyx insisted. She didn't back down from Juan Carlos who leveled a heavily hooded stare in Onyx's direction. "I'm sure you and Carmen will have another opportunity to celebrate, okay?"

Juan didn't immediately back down.

"Te prometo que ti veré más tarde," Carmen offered. "I promise I will see you later, okay?"

Juan Carlos turned to Carmen. His gaze was still as intense as when he stared at Onyx. Carmen softened her face, trying to appease him.

"I won't wait long," Juan Carlos said through clenched teeth.

"Espere diez años, amado," Carmen replied.

"Bueno, bueno mi amor," Juan Carlos conceded. "Call me later."

Carmen tried not to flinch when Juan Carlos leaned in to kiss her. She held her breath until his contact with her tightly closed lips were over. Carmen didn't fully exhale again until after Juan Carlos released her and started moving towards the door.

"Oh Dios mío," Carmen sighed.

"Oh my God is right," Onyx replied, exhaling with her. "How in the hell are you going to handle this?"

"I don't know," Carmen whined. "I need a drink to think."

"Sounds like a damn good idea."

The two ladies walked the short distance to the bar. Onyx went around the counter and picked up a bottle of tequila. She sat two shot glasses on the counter and filled them both. Onyx barely finished pouring before Carmen picked up the glass and threw the shot back. She sat the shot glass down hard and beckoned Onyx to fill it again. Onyx joined Carmen on the second shot and then the third. It was only after the last one did Carmen set the glass down and cradle her head in her hands.

"¿Qué demonios voy a hacer, Chica? What the hell am I going to do?"

"I don't mean to be mean Carmen, but I told you to tell him you were done before he got out."

"But you saw him, Onyx. Do you really think if I told him I had moved on while he was incarcerated that he just would have accepted it?"

"Probably not," Onyx acquiesced, pouring them both another shot.

"So, I am back to square one," Carmen moaned. "¿Qué demonios voy a hacer, Chica?"

Carmen and Onyx lifted their glasses and tossed back the last shot.

"I think I should call Egypt. Maybe he can help us think this through."

"I'm open to whatever at this point," Carmen conceded.

Chapter Eight

By the time Egypt arrived at the café, both Onyx and Carmen were feeling the effects of the alcohol. They weren't knock down drag out drunk, but they would lean without assistance.

"Did you bring the car, babe," Onyx asked as she leaned against the counter.

"I did," Egypt answered. "Can either of you walk?" Egypt tried not to laugh but the sight of his soon to be wife and her best friend hammered was funny.

"I can walk," Carmen said. She stood up from the seat and wobbled on her heels.

"Woo," Egypt groaned as he reached to catch Carmen. He helped Carmen sit back down.

"You two stay right here" Egypt instructed. "Don't move."

He waited until he received at least a nod from both of them before walking away. When Egypt returned, he was not alone.

"Oh no," Carmen sighed, seeing Grayson walking alongside Egypt. "Onyx, you didn't tell me he was here."

"Come on, beautiful," Grayson crooned as he wrapped his

strong arm around her waist and assisted Carmen to her feet. She was appreciative of Grayson's support, but even drunk, Carmen was completely embarrassed. She couldn't look into Grayson's eyes. She could only imagine what Grayson thought of her, what he was thinking of her as he assisted Carmen to the car. As they sat in the backseat, Grayson held on to Carmen as though he cared about her. Still, Carmen couldn't face him. She looked away, out of the passenger side window. When she felt Grayson's large hand cupping her head, encouraging her to rest on him, Carmen did, nestling her head on his shoulder. He still felt good to her. She still desperately cared about him.

There was still no clarity of thought for Carmen by the time the foursome arrived at Egypt and Onyx's place. She was still wobbly on her feet as the tequila did its work. Grayson was right there for Carmen, helping her inside and helping her to the couch.

"I'm gonna lay down for a minute," Onyx sighed. Egypt held her up as the two made their way to their bedroom.

"Will you stay with me," Carmen whispered. "I know I don't deserve it…"

"Shhh," Grayson whispered, cutting off whatever else Carmen had to say. He cradled Carmen in his arms, holding her close. Carmen rested on Grayson's chest, hearing his heartbeat in her ear; the consistent low drumming lulling her.

"I need to explain," Carmen sighed dreamily.

"Later," Grayson replied. "Right now, just rest."

He stroked her tresses, feeling the weight of her against him. That feeling was familiar. Grayson still liked how she felt in his arms. She did have some explaining to do. It would have been easy to jump to conclusions and call Carmen on the carpet about what he saw. But Grayson wasn't that kind of guy. He would give Carmen the opportunity to explain. He would give her the benefit of the doubt. Grayson didn't want what they were building to be lost based on presumption. He would hear her out. Still, seeing Carmen in the arms of another man, who acted as though he had a legitimate claim to her, was troubling. Grayson would have to deal with those feelings. At the moment, though, Grayson wasn't sure how.

Carmen woke up about an hour later. She didn't even realize she fell asleep. But being comforted by Grayson made it easy. He soothed her in a way no man had ever done before.

"Feeling better," Grayson asked, as he felt her waking in his arms.

"In a minute," Carmen replied. She excused herself and went to the restroom. She wanted to freshen up before breaching the subject of Juan Carlos with Grayson. She owed him an explanation. As Carmen examined herself in the bathroom mirror, she still didn't know what she would say. She wanted to be honest, but honesty could come with a cost; a cost Carmen wasn't willing to bear. Turning on the water in the sink, Carmen ruminated on the possibilities of what she would say. If she lied to Grayson, she would have to live with that lie and maintain it. That notion didn't sit well with Carmen as Grayson had been so forthright with her about so much. He deserved much more than a lie.

Carmen leaned down and splashed warm water on her face. She wanted to be as sober and in her right mind as possible when she spoke to Grayson. He deserved that, too. Carmen took a face towel from the small shelf and patted her face dry. She found some toothpaste and mouthwash and pulled herself together. By the time she was done, Carmen didn't feel nearly as hungover. There was a slight headache, but she would deal with that. Carmen didn't want her heart to break, though, if Grayson rejected her truth. That she couldn't deal with.

Her steps back to the living room were slow and contemplative. Carmen had such a feeling of dread that resonated in her gut, she almost didn't turn the corner to approach him. It would be so easy to retreat to the bathroom and pray Grayson got tired of waiting and leave. Carmen knew Grayson wouldn't do that though. He would sit there and wait until she returned, no matter how long it took. Grayson was just that kind of guy.

Carmen turned the corner to see Grayson sitting forward on the couch with his elbows resting on his knees. Carmen could see by the thick furrow of Grayson's brow that something was troubling him. Carmen had a really good idea what was bothering him. Carmen crossed the room, walking around Grayson instead of crossing over him. As she lowered herself on the couch next to Grayson, Carmen was nervous. She recognized that the depth of emotions she felt meant that Grayson was more than a casual acquaintance to her. Grayson had become something more; something Carmen didn't want to jeopardize.

"Thanks for being there for me Grayson," Carmen started. "I certainly don't deserve it."

"Why would you say that," Grayson asked. His body position didn't change which was a bit troublesome to Carmen.

"Because, you are such an incredible man, and," Carmen paused.

"And what, beautiful?" Grayson asked, turning around to face her.

He called me beautiful, Carmen thought. Maybe it was a habit. Maybe he had grown accustomed to calling her that, that Grayson didn't consider it under the circumstances. Maybe, he still meant it. Carmen hoped so.

"I like you, Papi," Carmen affirmed. "I like you probably more than I should. And I don't want you to go away from me because of what I need to tell you." It was a hard admission to make. Carmen felt like she was risking a lot, especially since she wasn't sure Grayson felt the same about her. But she had to take the risk. Carmen needed Grayson to know why this was so hard for her.

Grayson adjusted himself on the couch, so he came face to face with Carmen.

"Trust me," Grayson crooned. "Trust me, okay beautiful?"

"I'm scared, Grayson," Carmen sighed. She nervously ran her fingers through her hair and sat her hands in her lap clutching them tightly. Grayson placed his hand on top of hers, hoping to settle her obviously frayed emotions.

"Carmen, I am right here."

"It doesn't mean you're not going away," Carmen whispered.

Grayson could see Carmen struggling. He read it in her eyes, in her posture, in her voice.

"Trust me," Grayson reiterated, unfolding Carmen's clenched hands and taking them into his own.

Her shoulders lifted and fell as Carmen took in a deep settling breath. She closed her eyes and slowly opened them, doing her best to settle the churning in her gut. She had to trust him.

"The guy you saw me with earlier is a mistake from my past; a regrettable part of my younger life. Juan Carlos was my first love, who spent the last ten years in prison. We were close once, and for the first few years of his incarceration, I visited him. I was young and foolish and thought that he and I had something real. It took some time and maturity for me to realize that what we had was young love that had run its course. I don't even know if I could really call it love. I think it was more infatuation."

Carmen struggled to look at Grayson as she spoke. She felt his eyes taking her in, gazing at her in a way that usually made her smile. This time, Carmen didn't feel much like smiling. Even though it was her history, Carmen felt ashamed of it; ashamed of the girl she'd been in her youth. Logically, it wasn't fair to apply current level maturity and insight to the person she'd been before. But Carmen wasn't operating on logic. She wallowed in emotion.

"He wrote to me about a month ago to tell me he was getting out. It's my fault he showed up out of the blue today. Instead of me telling, Juan that I had moved on with my life, that I wasn't interested in rekindling our old relationship, I did nothing. I didn't know what to say. I didn't know how to tell him that I wasn't waiting for him."

Carmen fell silent, her eyes still averting Grayson's. She shared her truth; abbreviated, but the truth, nonetheless. The funky feeling in her stomach hadn't subsided though. It had only intensified as she waited on a response from Grayson. Carmen felt that sense of overwhelming anxiousness rise inside her.

"You really can't blame him," Grayson uttered.

"What?" Carmen asked, surprised by his commentary.

"You really can't blame him for wanting to rekindle what the two of you had," Grayson reiterated.

"I don't blame him," Carmen sighed. "Me culpa a mi mismo. I blame myself."

"But you shouldn't though," Grayson suggested. "I don't think it was the mature you who couldn't figure out a way to tell Juan that you were no longer interested. I think it was the little girl that used to be in love with this guy that didn't know what to say to let him down easily. But those are just my thoughts," Grayson offered.

Carmen sat back, digesting what Grayson said. She hadn't thought about it in that way; the reason for her hesitation.

"It makes so much sense when you explain it that way," Carmen replied. "Como llegaste a ser tan inteligente?"

Grayson chuckled. "Translation?"

Hearing Grayson ask that question again made Carmen laugh. It was a wonderful reminder of their connection.

"Translation; when did you get to be so smart?"

"I have no idea," Grayson laughed. "Glad you feel that way though."

"So, are you saying you understand," Carmen asked tentatively as their laughter died down.

"Sure, I understand why you didn't tell Juan, or whatever his name is. But,"

"Oh no, Papi," Carmen sighed squeezing his hands. "No but. Nothing good ever comes after but."

"But," Grayson repeated as he released Carmen's hand. His hand moved to cradle her face. "But, I wish that you trusted me enough to tell me about him before now."

Carmen's lips were downturned. Once again what Grayson said made perfect sense.

"I didn't intend to like you" Carmen whispered. "I didn't think you would be so likable. And when I realized I did like you, I didn't want to have to think about him. Maybe I was too busy enjoying the fantasy to think about my sad reality."

Grayson remembered what Carmen said about baggage. It made perfect sense now.

"Trusting people, not just you, but trusting people, in general, doesn't come easily to me. Most times, people are unworthy of your trust, but you don't figure that part out until it's too late. So, it's not that I don't trust you, specifically, it just takes me a while to trust generally."

Carmen searched Grayson's eyes to see if there was any understanding there.

"But," she began.

"Uh oh," Grayson muttered, turning slightly away from Carmen. "Nothing good ever comes after but," Grayson teased as he turned his attention back to Carmen.

"Don't tease me, Papi," Carmen fussed, reaching out and playfully pushing against his chest. "Eso no es agradable."

"But it's so much fun, Grayson chortled.

"Uhn," Carmen whined, pushing against Grayson's sculpted chest again.

"Okay, I'll stop" Grayson laughed, taking Carmen by her hand and pulling her into him. She hovered a breath away from his full lips. She could feel the warmth of his exhale against her skin.

"What were you going to say after the but," Grayson whispered against her luscious lips.

Carmen's eyes moved from Grayson's mouth to his eyes and back again. "I was going to say that I am learning to trust you, Grayson."

"I appreciate that," Grayson answered. "And given the brief time we've known each other, I understand why total trust at this point would be unrealistic."

"So, what are we going to do about the previously incarcerated one?"

Both Grayson and Carmen turned when they heard another voice in the room. Onyx and Egypt entered the room and sat down on the couch across from them.

"You guys have done enough, Onyx," Carmen replied. "I need to be the one to handle the previously incarcerated one." Carmen mimicked with air quotes.

"Are you sure about that," Egypt asked. "Was Juan incarcerated for a violent crime?"

"I think it was drug-related, not sure," Carmen replied. "Still, I own my mistake in not telling him sooner that I wasn't interested. I need to tell him now."

"What if he doesn't respond well," Onyx asked.

"Then I'll have to live with that, too" Carmen answered.

"But I don't know if I can live with that," Grayson interjected. "If he were to hurt you, beautiful," Grayson uttered.

"You do like me, huh," Carmen purred.

"Yes, I do," Grayson said, wrapping his arm around her. "More than you know."

"She knows now," Onyx quipped.

Grayson didn't bat an eye behind Onyx's comment. He meant what he said and was willing to stand behind it.

"So, what do we do," Egypt asked. "I'm with Turks on this one. If this guy reacts badly, we're not just going to stand aside and watch it go down."

The foursome sat with their thoughts, each trying to figure out the best possible way to address the situation.

"I understand your desire to handle this on your own, Carmen. If you do, though, it should be done in a public place so if Juan has a bad reaction, there could be somebody there to intervene," Onyx suggested.

"That's a good idea," Carmen replied. "The problem with that is, Juan is impatient. You saw that Onyx. He's going to want to see me immediately. I wouldn't be surprised if he was at my place waiting for me."

"How does he know where you live," Grayson asked.

"He said he always knew where I was, that he kept tabs on me."

"How though if he was locked up," Egypt asked.

"Juan Carlos has always been popular. Folks from the old neighborhood talk about him like he's a hero. Some of those same people know me," Carmen explained.

"Or your brothers," Onyx added.

"Culos tontos," Carmen mumbled. She looked to Grayson and smiled. "Dumb asses," Carmen translated. He smiled in return.

"If you think he'll be waiting for you, then you stay with me until this situation is resolved," Grayson suggested.

Onyx's brow lifted, and a smirk eased across her lips. She leaned into Egypt nudging his shoulder.

"You think that's best," Carmen asked Grayson.

Only if you're comfortable with it," Grayson answered.

"You can always stay here, Onyx offered.

"Or, you can stay with me," Grayson suggested again.

Carmen looked to Onyx. She was Carmen's barometer. Carmen frequently looked to Onyx for guidance; an example of what to do, instead of some of the things Carmen had done in the past. With a slight shrug of her shoulder and a gently delivered smile, Onyx offered her opinion on the matter. With that being said, Carmen turned her attention back to Grayson. Their eyes met. She was reminded why she felt herself falling for him. Carmen made her decision. She would stay with Grayson. He would keep her safe and happily distracted until her confrontation with Juan Carlos.

Chapter Nine

*O*nce the decision had been made, the foursome relaxed some and was able to focus on something other than Carmen's ex. They ordered in, had some dinner, and spent some time chatting and enjoying each other's company.

I could get used to this, Carmen thought to herself. Egypt was a wonderful man, and Carmen thought Onyx was incredibly blessed to find someone who loved her so much. She also thought Egypt to be quite blessed because Onyx was a gem. But Carmen never saw that kind of relationship for herself; not with someone as accomplished, as handsome, or as loving as a man like Egypt. But that was before Grayson. He was the possibility Carmen never thought she would have. She dated after Juan Carlos. But there was something about the men Carmen chose or that chose her that was Juan Carlos repackaged. She seemed to be in a rut or putting out the wrong kind of signal because Carmen kept attracting the same kind of man; the same as the man behind bars. Looking over at Grayson as he and Egypt enjoyed a glass of brandy at the bar, Carmen thought that for the first time, she was around a man who measured up to the kind of guy she always considered unattainable. She could get used to that.

"Do you think going to his place is a good idea?"

"It doesn't matter what I think, Carmen. It matters what you think," Onyx replied.

"I think I was just looking for some reassurance that I wasn't making a brain-dead move as I've done in the past."

"I hear you girl," Onyx answered. "But if I thought you were screwing up, you know I would tell you."

"Thanks, Onyx," Carmen replied. "I can always count on you to rein me in. Don't ever stop, okay?"

"I never will," Onyx answered.

It was late when the foursome parted ways. Carmen was glad to be on the back of Grayson's Harley again. After Juan Carlos showed up, Carmen wasn't sure she would ever get another chance. She held Grayson tightly as he maneuvered the bike down the interstate. Carmen closed her eyes as the cool of the night air stroked her face. That feeling of freedom never got old. She understood now why bikers biked. Carmen understood more why Onyx had a bike of her own. It wasn't so much about wanting to be like her man and do the things he did. Riding was about being able to experience the power and the freedom being on the bike offered, whenever she liked. Carmen could see that now. It was something she could feel. There was just something about it.

Carmen had been to Grayson's new home a time or two. She fully expected that they would be returning there. But Grayson went a different direction from the new house. They were headed downtown; the exact opposite of the suburban area the new house was located in. Grayson guided the bike into an underground garage. The headlight from the bike illuminated their route to a parking space. Grayson cut off the bike and helped Carmen to dismount. He rested their helmets on the handlebar and then lifted his frame from the bike.

"Did you need to make a stop before we went to your place," Carmen asked; accepting Grayson's extended hand.

"No," Grayson smiled. "This is my other place."

"How many places do you have," Carmen asked as they waited for the elevator to descend.

"A few," Grayson grinned.

"So more than two," Carmen asked amused.

"Yes, more than two."

The elevator door dinged as it opened. Grayson extended his free hand, ushering Carmen inside and then entered himself. Grayson turned a key that illuminated the P button on the board. Once it was lit, Grayson pressed it, and the elevator began to ascend.

"This was the first residential building I ever drew," Grayson said as the elevator stopped on the penthouse floor. When the doors opened into the apartment, Carmen was rendered speechless once again. Not only did Grayson have an amazing design aesthetic, but his sense of style was also impeccable. Carmen made her way out of the elevator and into the space. Grayson turned the lights on as he followed Carmen out of the elevator. Carmen's heels tapped lightly against the high-polished concrete floors. The deep eggplant curtains that puddled on the floor braced windows that spanned what seemed like the entire distance of the apartment. The curtains were open, and Carmen could see what looked like the entire city and beyond from her vantage point. Gray leather seating occupied the living space with lush throw pillows in deep purples and surprising greens for a pop of color.

Carmen was immediately drawn to the hallway. Pin lights illuminated beautifully abstract paintings that extended from one to the other. Grayson strolled behind Carmen as she appreciated his artwork.

"This piece is by Norman Lewis, famous African American artist from the 1970s," Grayson explained. "This next one is from Jean Michel Basquiat, a popular graffiti artist from the same time period. And this next one is from Black female artist Alma Thomas. It's called Iris, Tulips, Jonquils, and Crocuses. I think this one is my favorite."

Carmen paused as she listened to Grayson's description of the painting. Blues, oranges, yellows, and pinks were streaked vertically down the canvases. At closer inspection, what appeared to be simple lines were actually shapes that resembled flower petals.

"And this last one is by Beauford Delaney. He was born in 1901. Can you imagine what it was like having a creative heart during a time when our people were so oppressed? I can see how Mr. Delaney used his craft as an expression of his innermost feelings and thoughts."

"I can see that," Carmen replied. Carmen could see that in Grayson's designs; that his innermost feelings and thoughts were somehow translated first on the page and then in structural form.

"It has to be so rewarding to have your work appreciated," Carmen mused.

"It is I guess," Grayson replied. "But for most pure artists, its about the expression more than the acknowledgment."

"The art is about having a voice," Carmen said.

"Yeah," Grayson smiled.

"Maybe one day, I'll find my voice."

"You will, beautiful. You will."

They stood in the hallway for a while longer. Carmen found it hard to pull away from the artwork.

"It's late. Do you want to get settled?"

"All I have is the clothes on my back," Carmen replied.

"We can fix that," Grayson answered. "Wait right here."

Grayson strolled down the hallway fading from view. Carmen was fine with looking at the pictures. She smiled as she considered how much she learned about who Grayson was in the most innocuous ways. He had such depth and insight. She smiled wider when she thought about their first encounter; how she discounted him for being just a biker. Grayson proved over and over again that he was so much more than that. Carmen underestimated him; prejudged him. She wouldn't make that mistake again.

"I know it's probably not what you're used to, but I hope its okay," Grayson replied upon his return. He held up one of his t-shirts.

"It's fine, Papi," Carmen smiled.

"Good," Grayson crooned. "Let me show you where you'll be sleeping."

Carmen followed Grayson to the end of the hallway.

"Your bedroom is right here," Grayson said as he reached into the room and turned on the light.

"This is nice, Papi," Carmen replied, taking in the beauty of the space.

"Through there is your bathroom."

Carmen walked across the bedroom ad opened the door. The bathroom space was luxurious with a walk in shower and garden tub.

"This is not a bedroom, dear," Carmen sighed. "This rivals any suite in a five star hotel."

"Glad you like it," Grayson answered. "My room is on the other end of the hall. Just let me know if you need anything."

"I feel like I'm always saying thank you," Carmen sighed as she moved back in Grayson's direction. "And here I am saying it again. Thank you."

Carmen lifted onto her tiptoes and planted a soft kiss on Grayson's cheek. Her descent was slow as their bodies connected. Grayson felt a thump in his core as Carmen's voluptuous breast rubbed against his chest. Carmen felt a thump as intensely as Grayson did. Her body screamed out for him. Yet, Carmen took a step back and trailed her arms where her body had been before completely disengaging from him.

"Sleep well, beautiful," Grayson crooned.

"Sleep well, Grayson."

But Grayson didn't sleep well. In the shower, all he thought about was Carmen being just a few steps away. And when he laid down in his bed, his thoughts were of the one he craved the most. He wasn't the only one struggling. Carmen struggled in the shower as well. Grayson was everything she never thought she deserved, yet, he was right there. Grayson had stepped up for Carmen in ways no man had ever done before. He showed her a life and lifestyle she couldn't even imagine existed for people like her. He was honest and genuine and vulnerable at times without looking weak. Grayson was a real man; something she'd never experienced before.

Carmen lay in the bed wearing Grayson's shirt, trying to figure out how she would handle Juan Carlos. But Grayson's masculine scent remained in his shirt. Carmen lifted the collar of the shirt to her nose and inhaled. It was him. It was Grayson. All thoughts of Juan Carlos faded to the background as thoughts of Grayson filled Carmen's head. She tried to get comfortable in the bed and quiet the yearning she felt in her core. Squeezing her thighs tightly, Carmen tossed from one side of the bed to the other. She couldn't get comfortable. She couldn't stop thinking about Grayson.

Juan Carlos… He was back heavily, pushing himself into the forefront of her mind.

As though he somehow knew Carmen was thinking of someone else, pervasive thoughts of Juan Carlos clouded her mind. Carmen remembered how it felt to be in his arms again, how the touch that once set her soul on fire now made her flesh crawl. She didn't want to be with Juan Carlos, yet, Carmen didn't fully trust that if she told him that her feelings had changed, Juan Carlos would respond inappropriately, possibly violently. He might never leave her alone and move on with his life; allowing Carmen to move on with her own. She tossed and turned again. The conflictual feelings kept Carmen unsettled.

Carmen lifted herself from the bed. Maybe a glass of water or warm milk would help her settle. Carmen stepped out into the hallway; the cool of the concrete floor chilling her feet. Walking on tiptoe, Carmen moved towards the kitchen. She was careful to be quiet so as not to disturb Grayson. Once there, Carmen felt along the wall to find a light switch. When she turned the lights on, Carmen found the kitchen to be sleek but comfortable. She found a bottle of water in the refrigerator and retrieved it. The water was cool and refreshing but did nothing to quell the conflict that brewed in her mind. Carmen wanted to rest. As she made her way back down the hall, she paused at the divide. If she went left, Carmen would be back in the guest room. If she turned right, Grayson was there.

She didn't want to be alone. It was a risk Carmen was willing to take. She padded quietly down the hallway and stood in front of Grayson's door. Her heart beat so hard in her chest, she could feel the beat reverberate through her. Carmen took a deep breath and opened the door. Grayson heard the latch of the door release. His back was to the door. He didn't immediately respond. The light from the hallway illuminated Grayson's frame in the bed. She almost turned around and walked out, but she didn't.

"I don't want to be alone."

"You don't have to be, beautiful," Grayson said, turning over in Carmen's direction. Grayson lifted the covers, inviting Carmen in. Her steps were slow and measured as Carmen moved towards the bed. She sat down first and then lifted her feet from the floor, sliding in. Grayson draped the covers over her as Carmen settled in. When Carmen felt Grayson moving away, she reached out for him, taking his hand into her own. Grayson laid down behind Carmen, careful not to be presumptuous and breach her personal space.

The room was quiet; so quiet they could hear each other breathing. Carmen circled her thumb to the back of Grayson's hand. She eased their hands up higher, resting them on her chest. Grayson could feel Carmen's chest rise and fall. It was getting harder for Grayson to deny the yearning in his loins. Carmen eased back, eradicating the space between them. Her body was pressed flush against his. Carmen's breathing became deeper as she stroked the back of Grayson's hand, coaxing it open and placing his hand on the full of her breast. Carmen's breathing became labored. Grayson could feel the rise and fall of her chest even more as the pert of her nipple hardened under her hand. Carmen could feel the swell of Grayson's manhood against her ass and his warm breath against her ear as he spoke.

"Are you sure this is what you want," Grayson whispered. He was a man's man, and Carmen was the woman he desired. Yet, Grayson was aware of the fragile emotional state Carmen was in. He wanted her, desperately, but Grayson wanted it to be right, for Carmen and himself. He in no way wanted to take advantage of any vulnerability.

"Yes, Papi, please," Carmen panted. She pressed her ass against his thickness and undulated her hips. The thump in her yoni was real and strong. With permission granted, Grayson didn't hold back. He couldn't. Grayson leaned in, kissing and nibbling the lobe of her ear, Carmen gasped as the pull in her jewel heightened. The nibbles became tiny bites and hot kisses. Carmen moaned from the heated sensations coursing from her neck, down her back, and between her thighs. With a single kiss, Grayson brought out passions from within her she barely knew existed. All thoughts of her ex slipped from Carmen's mind as Grayson left a trail of heated kisses down her neck. Carmen felt the warmth from his muscle-toned body pressed up against hers. She melded into his folds; their two bodies becoming one.

"Kiss me," Grayson moaned from behind her. When he moved his strong arms, turning her, Carmen moved with him; looking up into his deep brown eyes, Carmen couldn't resist. Biting her bottom lip and feeling his manhood pressing between her wanton thighs, Carmen did kiss him, deep and long. The dance between their tongues sent shivers through Grayson as he felt an undeniable connection. Carmen was everything he ever desired in a woman.

Grayson's carnal desire drove him. He wanted to please Carmen in every way. Her lips tasted sweet and the suppleness of her body interlaced with his, sending a surge coursing through his loins. Carmen felt it too as she moved her body on top of Grayson. Their mouths remained entangled; her tongue exploring his and his exploring hers. The pulling sensation in Carmen's jewel could not be denied, and she straddled Grayson feeling his throbbing cock pressing against her womanhood. The moisture Grayson felt coming from her folds created a rage in his loins that could only be satisfied with Carmen's special touch. His manhood thickened as his dick pressed against her wanton womb. Reaching a hand down between her thighs, Carmen leaned slightly forward guiding Grayson inside her.

"Mmmm." Carmen groaned as she felt Grayson's swollen manhood move inside her. The fullness Carmen felt caused her eyes to roll to the top of her head. Grayson's hands moved to Carmen's ample hips, and he held her firm as he pulsed inside her. An animalistic groan escaped his lips as Carmen's body opened up and received him totally. With no space between them, Grayson thrust into her, hitting the top of her jewel and staying there long enough to send Carmen to her first heated climax. A stream of wet creaminess poured from her as Carmen's body gave in to Grayson's incredibly enticing touch.

The slow grind of Carmen's hips met the lift from Grayson's. There was a synergetic magnetism that connected more than just their bodies. Their hearts and souls were connected as well. Grayson leaned on his elbows, and Carmen leaned forward planting warm kisses from his forehead, down to the tip of his nose and then to Grayson's sensual lips. The change in position altered the way Grayson's dick pushed into her and Carmen bit down on his bottom lip when a wave of hot ecstasy pulsed through her. Grayson's lips moved from Carmen's down the base of her neck and to her full breasts. He took her pert nipple into his mouth and massaged her other swollen nipple between his thumb and forefinger. Carmen's head fell between her shoulders, and a tinge of heat surged in her yoni. Carmen couldn't resist having Grayson deeper inside her. She wanted all of him and wouldn't take anything less. Carmen slid up and down his stiffened pole; feeling his throb fill her to the brim. There was a quickening in her walls as Grayson's arms laced behind her, pulling him up, face to face with her. Their eyes connected as Carmen rode Grayson; the slap of her thighs against the muscle of his thighs echoing lascivious music between them.

"Papi," Carmen drawled as her entire body convulsed. Carmen felt the surge course through her, and it triggered a surge of his own as he called out her name. The rhythm between Grayson and Carmen quickened as well; the grind between them driving them both to the edge of ecstatic insanity.

"Beautiful," Grayson growled as the surge he felt deep inside threatened to spill over. Wrapping her arms tightly around his neck, Carmen rode Grayson hard and fast; losing all sense of time and space. They reached a new realm of connection where their hearts beat as one. The headboard banged rhythmically against the wall mimicking the clap between their thighs.

"Ah, Papi!" Carmen squealed as it all got to be too much in the most exhilarating way; the rush of emotions, the power of his fuck, the tremors of her own body in response to the thundering of his. The overload poured from Carmen and was met wholeheartedly by the overwhelming sensations Grayson felt. It was his nirvana. Carmen was his nirvana; unable to control himself or hold back any longer, Grayson's fingers dug into Carmen's back as the hot of his explosion poured from him. But that wasn't enough for Grayson. He wanted to make Carmen cum. He needed for her to be satiated and satisfied. He pushed, fucking her hard as her thighs clamped down on each side of him. Carmen's breasts bounced against his chest, and the sweat from her brow dripped onto him as Grayson pummeled her pussy; banging against her g-spot.

The purr that escaped Carmen's lips came from the depths of her soul as her body unleashed wave after wave of sweet nectar. Grayson refused to let her go, finding her lips and sucking them into his own as Carmen rode the climax of her life. Her body shook under his touch, and Grayson folded his arms around her, riding the waves of sensual pleasure with her. Carmen collapsed into him, and Grayson laid back. Sleep eventually found them, still holding each other.

Chapter Ten

"Everything go okay last night," Onyx asked as she and Carmen sat in her office in preparation for lunch service.

When Carmen didn't immediately respond, Onyx looked up from the paperwork on her desk.

"Uhn, Carmen, Chica," Onyx sighed. "You are absolutely glowing."

Carmen smiled as her cheeks flushed warmly.

"Guess I don't need to ask how things went last night," Onyx quipped.

"No, you don't," Carmen sighed. "Now if I can just get through the next few days, knowing Juan Carlos is lurking, I'll be okay; get back to my new life."

"I've got security on high alert," Onyx replied. "I know you said you wanted to handle this on your own, but I had to."

"I didn't think you would stay out of it," Carmen smiled.

"Whatever," Onyx replied. "Would you want me to?"

"No," Carmen answered. "I know you've got my back."

"And you know Turks and Egypt aren't going to stay out

of it either. They'll have the full legion of Down South Riders up in here if JC shows his ass."

"Grayson said something similar this morning," Carmen agreed. "That if I needed him, he would be right here."

"Feels good, doesn't it," Onyx asked.

"It does," Carmen replied. "To have someone to be there for you, yeah, it does feel good," Carmen continued. "Especially when it's for the right reasons."

"What do you mean?"

"Juan Carlos called himself being there for me, but it wasn't for the right reasons. He was trying to be a bad ass, make a name for himself. So, it really wasn't about me, it was about him in the end."

"Have you decided how you're going to handle it," Onyx inquired.

"Yes," Carmen answered. "I'm going to be honest with him. That's all I know to do. If there are repercussions, then I'll deal with them."

"I hope it doesn't come to that," Onyx replied.

"Me either," Carmen agreed.

Onyx fell quiet as she started to stack the papers on her desk.

"I've been thinking," Onyx said.

"What's up?"

"It's kind of along the same line, but hopefully that will become evident as we talk it through."

Carmen sat forward in her chair. She could see Onyx's wheels turning. Some of Onyx's greatest ideas started just like this, like the birth of Café Laquette. Carmen was intrigued.

"The government shutdown has gone on longer than it should have."

"Definitely," Carmen agreed. "So many people are suffering unnecessarily, it's crazy. And all for a freakin' wall. Es tan tonto," Carmen scoffed.

"I couldn't agree more. It is dumb and so uncalled for,"

Onyx replied. "And, I got to thinking, what can the café do to help?"

"What we do best," Carmen added. "Feed people."

"Exactly," Onyx chimed. "So, I thought, what if we did a luncheon for the furloughed federal workers and their families?"

"That's a great idea, Chica," Carmen agreed. "We could be there for the federal workers like you guys have been there for me."

"Exactly, and I don't want to wait too long to make this happen. The Lady Guardians are into helping the community. I would think they could get behind something like this, you know?"

"With your intimate connections to the President of the Dirty South Riders, I'm sure the guys would help out, too?"

"They would, Onyx replied. "Especially in helping us get the word out about the luncheon."

"That's good," Carmen replied. "But what about something more long term?"

"I see where you're going with that," Onyx answered.

"If we could provide food, they could take with them, can goods, produce, whatever we can come up with, I think would be a big help."

"That's a great idea," Onyx chimed. "Tre' has a bead on all the local pantries."

"And the growers from the markets," Carmen added.

They both paused.

"This could work," Onyx sighed.

"Yeah, I think it could."

"Okay," Onyx began. "I need to make a few phone calls. I need to reach out to Silk since she's the president of my chapter to see if the Lady Guardians will get behind this project. Maybe, if things go really well, we can get a Lady Guardian from the national chapter to come down, Cut, the vice president, or maybe even Justice, the national president."

"I can talk to Tre' to see what he thinks about reaching out to the pantries and the farmer's market," Carmen offered.

"That would help a lot," Onyx replied.

"What are we looking at as far as timeframe," Carmen asked as she got up from the chair.

"We can't wait too long," Onyx replied. "I would love to dedicate Sunday brunch to the workers. Too crazy?"

"That gives us a little less than a week," Carmen calculated. "It's crazy but doable."

"If we bust our asses," Onyx replied.

"Then let's make it happen boss lady," Carmen replied. "Nothing beats a failure but a try."

By the time the dinner rush was over, things were in high gear at the restaurant on more than one front. Onyx got in touch with Silk and the Atlanta chapter of the Lady Guardians was on board with feeding the furloughed families. There was even a chance that a representative from the national chapter would be in attendance. Egypt and the Down South Riders committed to spreading the word about the luncheon, passing out flyers and doing social media blasts. Tre' reached out to the pantries who were more than willing to help, and several representatives from the farmer's market were very happy to make donations. Carmen played her role coordinating the donations and determining a point of contact for the furloughed workers in the area.

It was good for Carmen to keep busy. Focusing on

someone other than herself in their time of need made Carmen feel purposeful. Carmen got to use skills she didn't use regularly. Organizing and coordinating didn't give Carmen much time to think about Juan Carlos. She was grateful for that. Carmen was even more excited when she heard the rumbling of several motorcycles pulling up to the restaurant. Even before Grayson came into view, Carmen knew he was there. A smile danced at the corners of Carmen's lips as she walked towards the window. Watching Grayson dismount his bike gave her a thrill. He was so strong and robust and looked hell-a-good in his dark denim jeans, white tee shirt, and black leather jacket.

Several of the bikers entered the restaurant, but Carmen only had eyes for one.

"Papi," Carmen sang as she sashayed into Grayson's open arms.

"Hey beautiful," Grayson said, wrapping his thickly corded arms around her taut waist. Grayson lifted Carmen off the floor, twirling Carmen in a small circle.

"Uhn, I remember this slide," Carmen purred as she descended the length of him.

"This is what got you in trouble for last night," Grayson drawled in her ear.

"I like trouble," Carmen sang.

"Me too."

The titillating kiss the two exchanged was enough to warrant catcalls from Turks biker brothers.

"Turks! Turks! Turks!"

Grayson smiled against her lips. And to pander to his friends, Grayson dipped Carmen, who was more than willing to play along and leveled Carmen with another sizzling kiss.

"Get a room," Onyx teased as she wanked into the arms of her man.

"We thought we'd come by, just in case," Egypt said and then kissed Onyx on the cheek.

"Thank you, baby," Onyx sighed. "And the media blitz?"

"Going well," Egypt explained. "We also got a few radio plugs from a fellow biker from another legion who just happens to be a DJ."

"Oh, babe! You are the best," Onyx sang as she laced her arms around Egypt's neck.

"I try," Egypt crooned.

They were all so caught up in their own entanglements that neither of them noticed Juan Carlos entering the establishment. But he noticed Carmen in the arms of another man. Juan Carlos was immediately infuriated. The heaviness of his footfalls didn't go unnoticed, though. Carmen caught sight of Juan Carlos approaching in her periphery.

"He's here," Carmen sighed.

"Do you want me to handle it," Grayson asked as he still held Carmen in his arms.

"No, Papi," Carmen replied. "I need to do this myself. But thank you though." Carmen leaned in and kissed Grayson softly on the cheek, but her eyes never left Juan Carlos.

As she eased from the comfort of Grayson's arms, Carmen walked towards Juan Carlos. She could see the flare of Juan's nose and his fists clenched by his sides.

"Let's talk outside," Carmen said, stepping in front of Juan Carlos. His jaw was tight, and his breathing was labored. She could see Juan working himself into a frenzy. Carmen refused to back down though. She placed her hand on Juan Carlos' arm and refocused his attention to her.

"Necesito que salgas conmigo, Juan."

Juan Carlos stood firm refusing to move. His hooded stare in Turks direction didn't go unnoticed. Several of the bikers stood to their feet, ready for whatever. Turks didn't turn to face Juan Carlos. He refused to give Juan the benefit of his attention.

"Juan Carlos, please," Carmen insisted, holding his arm firmer. "Come outside with me." Carmen stepped directly into Juan's line of sight and refused to move until she captured his eyes. Juan had no choice but to look at Carmen. Their eyes connected. Although her voice stern, there was still a familiar softness in Carmen's eyes that soothed the beast raring up in Juan Carlos.

"Ven, Juan Carlos, come."

His feet finally started moving. At first Juan's steps were reluctant and he looked back over his shoulder more than once. But Juan was finally able to detach enough from what was happening inside to focus on moving outside with Carmen.

"Who the fuck is that, Chica?"

"That, Juan Carlos, is my new friend who I like very much."

It was a bold statement, but Carmen knew in order to do this, she couldn't appear weak; like the same girl Juan knew years ago. She could tell by the surprised look on Juan Carlos' face that he didn't expect what he was getting from Carmen.

"What the hell do you mean, Carmen?"

"I should have said something to you a long time ago," Carmen began. "I just thought once I stopped visiting, that you would get it."

"Get what?"

"That I am not the same, Juan! That ten years have passed when you were locked up, and I was out here, trying to live my life. That I don't love you anymore," Carmen's frustration was starting to show. But that wasn't the way to get her message across to Juan Carlos. Carmen took a long, slow breath before continuing. "I haven't loved you for a long time."

Juan's nose flared again, and his jaw set tightly. Carmen's eyes fell to Juan's hands again, and she watched him open and close his fists repeatedly. He took a few steps away from Carmen and then methodically returned. The fierceness in Juan's eyes hadn't diminished. That didn't stop her though. Carmen thought about what she had with Juan versus what her life was like now; her job, her friends. She also considered the possibilities with Grayson. Carmen could not afford to back down.

"For you to have an expectation that after all these years I would sit idly by and wait for you is not fair. Me waiting is about you. It has nothing to do with me," Carmen reasoned. "That would be like I was locked up just like you Juan and I didn't commit a crime."

Juan Carlos didn't like what he was hearing, but Carmen didn't care.

"So, what am I supposed to do, huh? Just let you walk out on me?"

Carmen heard the challenge in his voice, but she also heard some pain. Turks didn't stand idly by why Carmen talked with her ex. He stood at the window watching. Turks wanted to respect Carmen's decision to handle it on her own, but he didn't trust the ex. When Juan Carlos clenched his fists or step too aggressively in Carmen's direction, Turks' fists clenched too, and he started more than once to make his presence known. Turks' feelings for Carmen were undeniable, and no ghost from her past was going to interfere with that.

"You walked out on me a long time ago, Juan."

"But I love you. We belong together. It's always been you and me," Juan insisted.

"Juan that was a long time ago. It was young love. I'm not that girl anymore."

"You still look like that girl to me," Juan crooned, reaching his hands out to touch Carmen on the waist. When she slapped his hand away, Juan looked stunned. His brows lifted and his eyes widened. Juan drew back. Carmen's eyes narrowed, and she clenched her fists despite the erratic thumping of her beating heart. This time it was Juan who saw Carmen's closed fists. Any other time he would have been dismissive of her affront to his masculinity. He would check Carmen and put her in her place. That's how Juan would have responded. Then, he looked in Carmen's eyes. Juan Carlos really looked; not at what he expected to see, but what was there. Her words were harsh, and her posture was firm. She'd always been sassy, a smart ass. But after she said something challenging to Juan Carlos, Carmen used to smile and make light of the situation; doing whatever she could to stay on Juan's good side. This time, though, Carmen's eyes were resolute. She wasn't backing down. She wasn't laughing or trying to soften it up. Carmen was different.

"I'm not that girl anymore, Juan," Carmen reasoned. "You need to move on."

Juan took a step back from Carmen, shaking his head.

"Te amo, mi amor," Juan said between clenched teeth.

"If you love me like you say you do, then you will let me go."

"What if I refuse?"

"You don't have a choice," Carmen replied. "I choose now."

Even though adrenaline pumped hard through Carmen's veins and the beat of her heart pounded in her chest, she bravely pivoted on her heels and turned her back on Juan. She had to make this goodbye final whether he liked it or not. Juan Carlos didn't like it. He stood there, watching the woman he loved, the woman he pinned all his hopes on, start to walk away. Carmen didn't hear the animalistic growl that came from Juan Carlos' lips over the sounds of the street. Carmen felt a gripping hand to her forearm that stopped her forward motion. Her eyes instinctively dropped to the arm but were unable to linger as her head was thrust back and her neck pinched tightly against the strength of Juan's arm around her neck. Carmen's air supply was immediately snatched away, and she clawed at the thing choking her.

"Tu eres mio!" Juan Carlos hissed hotly against Carmen's cheek; sprays of his hot breath dousing her flesh. "You are mine!"

Carmen sputtered, trying to get air into her lungs that burned in her chest from deprivation. She clawed so hard into Juan's flesh that Carmen drew blood. Juan winced from the stinging pain and then smiled.

"I love it when you're feisty, mi amor."

Juan Carlos planted a wet, breathy kiss to Carmen's cheeks.

Carmen's eyes were wide, and her head was foggy. Kicking her feet and writhing her body, Carmen fought to get out of Juan's clutches. Hot tears pressed against the back of her eyes and started to spill onto her cheeks; cheeks that were losing color. Turks swift movement out of the café caused his fellow brothers to turn their attention outside. They moved as a unit, stepping out of the restaurant and onto the sidewalk. When Egypt stopped mid-sentence and moved out quickly, Onyx's brow raised and her feet started to move, following Egypt.

"Carmen," Onyx whispered as she hustled to the front door. Onyx could feel a leap in her chest and a pang in the pit of her stomach.

Brothers from the Dirty South Riders spilled onto the sidewalk surrounding Juan Carlos and Carmen. Turks kept his eyes trained on Carmen.

"Let her go," Turks bellowed. His voice was loud and brash, but for Carmen, Turks eyes were soft and reassuring. When he turned his gaze momentarily to Juan Carlos, Turks eyes were icy. He took a decisive step towards Carmen and Juan. Turks was careful though. He didn't want Juan to hurt Carmen even more.

"Vete a la mierda, estupido!"

Turks didn't care what Juan said. He just needed Juan Carlos to let the love of his life go. Juan started to backpedal, taking Carmen with him. Turks moved forward, closing the distance. He could see how frightened Carmen as and it pricked Turks heart. Carmen wanted to call out to Turks, but her words were cut off. She kept working though, doing her best to get her fingers between her neck and Juan's arm.

"Motherfucka, I said let her go," Turks hissed steadily moving forward, eradicating the space between him and Juan Carlos. Juan's eyes moved from one side to the other seeing the bank of men standing around. Egypt stood behind Turks ready for battle.

"Carmen! Oh my God," Onyx groaned. It was a distraction. Juan Carlos stumbled and then quickly tried to regain his footing. That was hard, though, as Juan bumped into a wall of angry men, stopping him short. Juan's imbalance was enough to give Carmen a chance. And she took it. His arm loosened and the brothers of Dirty South took the opportunity to grab hold of him, giving Carmen the chance to get free. She stumbled towards Turks, who was right there to keep her from falling. Carmen still couldn't catch her breath, inhaling deeply trying to compensate for the lack of oxygen. She coughed violently as fresh air poured into her lungs.

"I gotchu, babe," Turks said reassuringly, scooping her up into his arms. Onyx flew to Carmen's side. As always, she wanted to be there for her friend. Onyx's eyes were filled with tears as she reached for Carmen. The look on Turks face said he had some unfinished business to attend to.

"Come on, sweetie," Onyx encouraged as Turks gingerly released Carmen into Onyx's hands.

"I'll be right there," Turks whispered reassuringly to Carmen. Once the ladies were safely out of the way, Turks turned his attention to the problem. Turks brothers still held Juan Carlos who flayed unsuccessfully to get away. The brothers weren't having that until Turks was ready for him. When Turks turned to face Juan, the brothers pushed Juan forward. But he quickly fell back as Turks left hook and right cross rocked Juan Carlos' face. Bright red blood spewed from Juan's nose as his eyes teared from the brutal sting. Juan fell back, but the brothers refused to let him fall. Turks stepped decisively forward again, lifting Juan in his collar and drawing him close.

Turks gaze was like daggers cutting through Juan Carlos. Turks pulled Juan close, so he didn't miss what Turks had to say.

"If you ever come around Carmen again," Turks spat, snatching Juan in his collar. Turks didn't even blink as blood splattered. Juan had a hard time looking Turks in the eye. But he refused to look like a punk, even those Juan's eyes continued to water. "I will kill you," Turks threatened between clenched teeth. Forcefully, he let Juan go, releasing him. But instead of falling against the wall of bikers again, Juan fell hard to the concrete sidewalk, leaving another splay of blood as his shirt raised and the concrete scraped his flesh. Turks stepped forward one last time; his shadow looming darkly over Juan. Turks brothers stood with him, and they watched as Juan Carlos tried to get up. Carmen had been watching the whole time. She saw how Turks stood up for her, and the brothers supported their own. She broke through the line of bikers to get to Turks.

"Papi, mi héroe," Carmen exclaimed as she laced her arms around Turks neck, kissing him feverishly on the cheek. He held her in the strength of one arm, as he kept his eyes on Juan who was struggling to get up.

"I don't think we're gonna have any more problems out of this one, bro," one of Turks fellow bikers barked.

"Me either," another agreed.

"Come on, Papi," Carmen encouraged, lifting her hand and inclining Turks chin in her direction. His nose was still flared, and Carmen could feel the tension in his body. Carmen gained his eyes as she softly stroked the side of Grayson's face, bringing him back to her. she watched as his features softened; the tension releasing from Grayson's jaw and his eyes warming over. Confidently, Turks turned his back on Juan Carlos again. His brothers filled in the gap, creating a barrier between them.

Carmen held on to Grayson as they made their way into the café. The Dirty South Riders had Grayson's back, and he had hers.

Grayson was right there, placing a loving hand to her back. Carmen shook her head quickly as she tried to level her breathing. She was scared; afraid that she wouldn't be able to stand up to Juan Carlos. But she did. She did, and Grayson did with her.

"Surprisingly, I am fine, Papi."

"And you," Carmen asked.

"Good," Grayson sighed, pulling Carmen into a warm, firm hug. "I just couldn't let him do you like that," Grayson sighed. "Cause if anything more happened to you," Grayson whispered against Carmen's ear.

"Then what," Carmen asked pulling away enough to look Grayson in the eyes.

"Then I don't know what I would do," Grayson rasped.

"And why is that," Carmen implored gazing into Grayson's dark, brooding eyes.

"Because," Grayson began; his eyes dreamy and his tone sincere. "I think I'm falling in love with you."

Carmen lifted her hand to Grayson's handsomely chiseled face and traced a single finger along his jawline, stopping against Grayson's lips. She leaned in and elevated on her toes; replacing her finger with her full lips kissing him softly.

"Me estoy enamorando de ti."

"Translation," Grayson asked, kissing Carmen between syllables.

Carmen giggled, letting her head drop between her shoulders. When she lifted her head and returned her gaze to Grayson, the smile on her lips remained.

"I think I'm falling in love with you, too."

Chapter Eleven

ONE WEEK LATER

Several motorcycles lined the front of Café Laquette. The Lady Guardians and the Down South Riders turned out in full force for the event. Even Cut from Nationals was present. There was an impressive crowd for the *Let's Eat* luncheon. More than a hundred furloughed workers and their families were there to enjoy a four-course meal prepared by café staff. A live band who donated their time were there to entertain the families, and there were even a few clowns, blowing balloon animals for the kids. The families were treated like royalty with full waiter service, linen napkins, and fine china. And to make sure that each family could eat past the event, there were boxes of food and fresh produce the families could take with them.

"This turned out really well, Chica," Carmen said as she gave Onyx a one-armed hug. "You should be proud of yourself."

"I'm proud of everyone who helped," Onyx replied. "I couldn't have done this alone."

"It's time, babe," Egypt said as he walked up to the duo.

"I hate public speaking," Onyx whined quietly as she felt her nerves start to stand on edge.

"You got this, Mami," Carmen encouraged.

"Ladies and gentleman, please help me welcome to the stage, owner and proprietor of Café Laquette, Ms. Onyx Malone!"

"Soon to be Onyx Anderson," Egypt replied. Giving Onyx a good luck kiss to the cheek, Egypt joined the rest of the audience in applauding for Onyx as she took the stage.

"Thank you, everyone," Onyx began after taking the microphone into her hand. "I just want to take a moment to thank everyone who made this special occasion possible. Thank you to Kai Jefferson, president of The Atlanta Chapter of the Lady Guardians and all our wonderfully supportive legion members. Thank you, lady bikers," Onyx sang. Thank you to our special guest, Cut, National Vice President of the Lady Guardians. I also want to thank the members of The Dirty South Riders who were instrumental in getting the word out about Let's Eat. Thank you to all the local pantries and farmers from the fresh markets who didn't hesitate to give freely to our honored guests. Thank you to our entertainers who willingly donated their time and talent. And last but not least, thank you to my staff at Café Laquette. Guys, when I came up with this idea not more than one week ago, you didn't hesitate to do whatever it took to make it happen without one word of complaint. I couldn't be prouder of how you all pitched in, worked overtime and did more than what was necessary to ensure our honored guests felt just that honored."

There was another roaring round of applause from all those in attendance. Onyx continued as the applause died down.

"And to our families, thank you for being here. Without you none of this makes sense. I want you all to know that collectively we support you and we are here for you. We all may have our opinions about the furlough, but at the end of the day, the pervasive effect is hardship to those who are no longer being paid for the work they do and their families. The hardship is unfair and unnecessary. We hope that what we've done today, helps to ease that burden, just a little bit. Thanks for being here."

As Onyx left the stage, Silk and Cut met her there.

"Nice job, Midnight," Cut said, calling Onyx by her biker name.

"Thanks so much for coming, Madame Vice President. It means a lot," Onyx replied.

"It was my pleasure," Cut smiled. "You know one of our primary tenants is making a positive impact in the community, and this luncheon definitely does that."

"I'm definitely impressed with how quickly you pulled everything together," Silk observed.

"Thanks, Madame President, but that was not all me," Onyx answered. Onyx reached over and tapped Carmen on the shoulder, bringing her into the conversation.

"This is Carmen Rodriguez, chief organizer for this event. Carmen, this is Silk and Cut."

"Nice to meet you ladies," Carmen smiled.

"You did a great job, Carmen," Cut smiled. "Organizing an event on this level in such a short period of time, that's impressive."

"Thank you, Cut," Carmen sang.

"You know, we can always use impressive women in our club," Silk commented. "Onyx, I'm surprised you haven't invited Carmen to a meeting."

Onyx turned to Carmen to gauge her response. The smile on Carmen's face said it all.

"I think I will," Onyx replied.

"Good, hope to see you soon," Silk replied.

Carmen and Onyx watched as the two lady bikers walked away.

"I think they like me," Carmen mewed.

"Would you really go with me, to a meeting?"

"I don't even have a bike," Carmen laughed.

"What's all this about," Grayson chortled as he and Egypt joined the ladies near the stage.

"Carmen just got invited to a Lady Guardian's meeting," Onyx replied.

"And I was just telling Onyx, that I don't have a bike. How am I going to be a bicker chick without a bike?"

"We can fix that," Grayson smiled.

"Squee!" Onyx chimed. "This is going to be so awesome, the four of us cruising down the highway. It's going to be awesome!"

One Month Later

Turks and Egypt waited outside the Lady Guardians meeting. Carmen had been vetted a week or so before, and if all went to plan, Carmen would emerge from the meeting a member of the Lady Guardians. Inside, Onyx was as nervous as Carmen was. She remembered what it felt like sitting in the center of the circle, waiting to hear whether she made the cut. But Onyx was also excited. She and Carmen were already very close. If Carmen was confirmed, though, they would be more than best friends. They would be sisters on a level many never had the opportunity to experience.

All the Lady Guardians of the Atlanta Chapter were present and wearing their traditional gray vests; President Kai

'Silk' Jefferson, Vice Missy 'Wheels' Washington, Treasurer, Fallon 'Breezy' Butler, Chapter Secretary, Jillian 'Wiggles' Lowe, and Sergeant at Arms, Tangela 'Tootie' Rawls. The room was quiet as all the members stood in a circle around the probate. Carmen was nervous, but just like Onyx, she was excited too. Carmen was excited about the possibilities.

"Carmen Rodriguez," Tootie began. "As you know, the women of the Lady Guardians are not just lady bikers. We are not just women who ride with men who bike. We are influencers and change agents; women committed to our families, our communities and our sisterhood. We are strong, powerful, complex women who move in this world through various occupations. But we move as a unit; sisters bonded by our oaths, our commitments, and our determination to make a difference. And, we ride bad ass bikes. Do you understand?"

"Yes, I do," Carmen replied.

"Stand to your feet, Carmen Rodriguez," Tootie instructed.

Carmen stood nervously to her feet.

"Are you willing to be a part of this sistership, this bond that extends past blood," Tootie questioned.

"Yes," Carmen replied.

"Are you willing to support and contribute intellectually to the maintenance and development of the charities and charitable endeavors we undertake?" Tootie asked.

"Yes, I am," Carmen answered.

"And are you willing to uphold the bylaws of the Lady Guardians and above all else, be a respectable pillar and example in the community," Tootie inquired.

"Yes," Carmen replied. "Yes, I am."

A wide smile spread across Onyx's lips. Carmen smiled too, as she understood that she belonged to a group that was much bigger than one individual. Carmen understood that she was a part of a group that would expand what possibility looked like.

"As a sisterhood, we decide what we think the most appropriate nickname is for our members," Wheels began. "The name we've selected for you, Carmen Rodriguez, our newest member is, Spice."

Carmen's eyes widened, and her hands flew to her mouth covering the broad smile she wore. After Wheels announced Carmen's new name, she lifted the gray leather vest with the club patch and Carmen's rider name etched in cursive.

"Midnight, would you do the honors," Wheels asked.

"I would love too," Onyx replied, stepping into the circle. Onyx walked over to Wheels and retrieved Carmen's vest. She then approached Carmen and helped Carmen put her LG vest on.

"Congratulations, Spice," Midnight smiled as the two exchanged a warm hug.

"Welcome to the Lady Guardians, Spice," Kai announced as the entire sisterhood congratulated Carmen.

"Thank you all so much," Carmen smiled.

When the ladies emerged from the meeting, Grayson could see the wide smile on Carmen's face. He strolled in her direction.

"Congratulations, beautiful," Grayson drawled as he leaned down and kissed Carmen on the forehead.

"Thank you," she replied. "But when we ride, please call me Spice."

Grayson's eyes dropped to Carmen's vest.

"Uhn, okay, Spice it is," Grayson chortled. "I'm happy for you, babe."

"Me too," Carmen sang.

"And to celebrate your membership in the biker world, I've got a little something for you," Grayson said, reaching out and taking Carmen by the hand. Egypt took Onyx's hand as well as they strolled across the parking lot.

"This one is for you."

Carmen followed Grayson's line of sight, and her feet

stopped moving instantly.

"Papi! You didn't," Carmen exclaimed.

"Yeah, he did," Onyx chimed.

"Dios mio," Carmen screamed as she approached the bike.

"This is for me?"

"Yes, beautiful," Grayson replied, stepping up beside her. "She's all yours."

"Ella es hermosa," Carmen sighed as she slowly padded around the 2019 V Star Custom Classic cruiser in steel gray with hot pink and black piping.

"Ella es hermosa," Carmen sang as she laced her arms around Grayson's neck. "She is beautiful."

The heat of the kiss between the two was hot enough to make Egypt and Onyx turn away like they were invading a private moment.

"Get a room already," Onyx mumbled.

"I heard that," Carmen giggled as her and Grayson's lips separated.

"Come on beautiful, cruise with me," Grayson smiled.

"I would love, too."

The End

THANK YOU SO MUCH FOR READING CRUISIN'. I WOULD REALLY appreciate it, especially if you enjoyed the story, to leave a review on Amazon and Goodreads. For Indie authors, reviews are the lifeblood of our work. They give other readers insight into the story and greater visibility for the authors. Thanks in advance and I hope you will continue reading the Moore series with me!

And here is the first chapter of Wyked by Chelle Ramsey!

Chapter Twelve

LOVE'S TRAIN

*B*ristol reviewed her article one final time before submitting it to her editor for final edits. She stared out of the window of her office at the amazing view of Woodruff Park in downtown Atlanta. College students, businessmen and women, panhandlers, and older men playing chess intermingled together in an unconventional and diverse blend. Bristol saw the people moving around living their lives, but it did not penetrate her brain. Her mind was on the piece she had just written for the article and how it related to her own life.

As a columnist for Uzuri magazine, she created pieces about relationships in the African-American population, encouraging her readers to believe there was still a thing as true love in the black community. She highlighted long-term relationships among average couples, relationship issues, deal breakers, and special acts that fostered romance in the relationship.

Uzuri was created by romance author, Laci Adair as a means of promoting authors, relationships, and finances in the black community. She allowed her writers free reign of their topics, so creative control was pretty much a given. Her only requirement was that the topics aligned with what the readers expected.

Bristol's column, *Upendo Nyeusi*, translated to "black love," in Swahili reached out to thousands of subscribers weekly. Her topics were inspirational, thought-provoking, and sometimes controversial. Each of her readers gained a life message after reading any of her columns. This latest one had her thinking about her own relationship.

A buzzing sound drew Bristol's attention away from her thoughts. Picking up the black handset to her right, she answered it without checking the ID.

"Patton, hon, I finished this article and sent it to Drew," she said, of her editor. "What's up?"

"Joe just called and left a message that he would not be able to get away for lunch. He said he was caught on an important conference call and he would call you later," Patton, her assistant explained.

Bristol frowned, wishing she had not forgotten her charger at home that day. Her cellphone had died earlier that morning. She wanted to speak to Joe, needing some reassurance at the moment. Coming up with a better idea, she shrugged and replied, "It's okay. I need to leave early anyway," she muttered, glancing at the time before hanging up the extension.

She had been invited to do a feature story on a power couple in the Atlanta black business community. Onyx and Egypt Anderson had recently married and were the epitome of a strong, loving relationship among black couples.

Egypt had been on an outing with his motorcycle club, and the need for nourishment had led him to her restaurant, Café Laquette in Little Five Points and the two had been inseparable since. She was a restaurateur and he owned a construction company. He created beautiful communities, including subdivisions specifically designed for those who were financially challenged. As president of the Dirty South Riders, he had introduced her to the motorcycle club she was now a member of, the Lady Guardians.

Bristol had been hearing a lot about the female motorcycle club taking the country by storm. Their charitable donations, community service, and commitment to righting the wrongs they encountered in their communities brought a spotlight on them. She was scheduled to do an interview with them this weekend during their club anniversary. The banquet was being held in downtown Atlanta, so there was no travel required for Bristol, but she needed to prepare for her meeting with the ladies.

Bristol composed one final email, clicked send, and then powered down her laptop. Satisfied that she was all caught up on everything and could leave out early for the weekend, she stuffed her laptop in its case, grabbed her Coach bag, and her keys and sunglasses. She and Joe were supposed to have lunch today because she would be too busy this weekend to keep their date night.

They had been trying to bring the spice back into their relationship after suffering a tragic loss. Only six months earlier, the two had lost their infant daughter. Camden had caught a staph infection and never recovered from it. The first sign that something had been wrong was the fever she contracted that would not break with Tylenol. Taking her to the ER one night, neither parent knew that they would never return home with their eight-month-old daughter.

The loss had taken its toll on their relationship, with Bristol moving out of the house they shared into an apartment of her own. She had pushed the wedding back by another year, but she wasn't certain she would be ready then either.

Determined she would do something to surprise him, she headed to the home they once shared. Joe was a financial planner and often worked from home, as she knew he was doing this day. Bristol stopped to pick up lunch for them at their favorite little Thai restaurant because she knew when he was caught up with work, he seldom stopped to eat. She did not plan to keep him for long, just long enough to make sure that he ate before she left. And how much time he could spare would determine what all he ate that afternoon, she thought, with a saucy grin on her face.

Bristol would make a small detour by her apartment before heading to Joe's house.

***

BRISTOL INSERTED THE KEY INTO THE LOCK AND LET HERSELF in. She strutted to the kitchen, the click of her stiletto heels silenced by the thick Berber carpet along the hallway, her hips sashaying with each step. She knew once Joe saw her in her black cut-out open back bandage dress, he would forget all about his phone conference, especially when he realized she was wearing nothing underneath.

She knew that her focus had not been on her man as it should have lately. It was hard managing the grief and depression that came with such a loss while trying to keep the spice in their relationship. After writing her article, she committed herself to the idea of reigniting the flames that had died down between them.

Bristol paused in the hallway, before turning around and heading back to the kitchen. Setting the food on the breakfast nook, she walked to his mini wine cellar and removed a bottle of Cabernet. She grabbed two glasses and made her way to his office, deciding she would come back for the food.

Finding it, empty, she chose to sneak further down the hall, wondering if he was just working in his bedroom like he oftentimes did. The light from the door at the end of the hallway confirmed her thoughts. Standing in the doorway, the wine glasses and bottle of wine fell from her hands onto the wood floor, crashing and sending shards of glass all around her, while wine splashed onto the walls, her outfit, and a nearby dresser.

Bristol screamed louder than she ever had before at the horror that lay before her.

Joe was lying on his back in the bed, head bent at an angle, his mouth a grotesque depiction of terror the rest of his nude body hidden underneath the woman who sat halfway astride him. They clearly had been in the midst of a sexual act when someone had decided to bring their illicit affair to an end.

Compelled to move forward by some unseen force, Bristol stepped into the room, the sound of her heels crunching the glass underneath her, unheard by her ears. The woman's eyes were closed. Both bodies postured in a macabre depiction of pleasure. Her back was to the doorway suggesting she had been oblivious to the audience of their intruder, who was privy to their private and indecent moment.

A gamut of emotions rolled through Bristol at the recognition that the woman Joe was having an affair with was none other than his former girlfriend, Rachel Stringer. Who had committed this gruesome crime? Who else had known about their affair, because Bristol surely hadn't? She felt herself growing sick, the morning's breakfast roiling inside her belly, bubbling up to her throat, leaving an acidic trail behind as she turned and ran into the bathroom and threw up all over the floor.

Hands on her knees, chest heaving, eyes stinging, she tried to block out the scene she had just witnessed. But it was impossible. Shock and hurt ran a rampant and competitive race throughout her to see which would come through at the finishing line first.

How could he do this to her? Did he not realize how much she loved him? Did he not understand the devastation his acts could create? How long had this been going on between them, or was this some one-time thing?

On shaky legs, Bristol walked to the sink, gripping the cold ceramic in her hands as she tried to quell the fear and disgust churning in her stomach. She had no idea who had done this, or even if they would come back again. For all she knew, that person could still be in the house. With that thought in mind, she ran into the bedroom, locked the door and grabbed Joe's house phone from the night table. Careful not to allow her eyes to look their way again, she rushed back into the bathroom and locked that door, as well.

Dropping on the edge of the Roman tub, she dialed nine-one-one, refusing to wait another moment to discover if she was alone.

"Nine-one-one dispatch, how may I assist you?"

"Uh…my…I need…"

"Hello, ma'am. How can I help you?"

"They're dead…" she cried hysterically into the phone.

"Who's dead, ma'am?" the operator asked.

"He…he's dead, and she's dead. My…I need the police here right away," she stammered.

Bristol was uncertain of any other questions that were asked of her, she only knew eventually she got off the phone and released a loud wail from deep within her body.

She cried until the police and ambulance arrived. She was inconsolable as they made their way throughout the house, conducting their investigation. Shortly after their arrival, she began crying again when she heard one of the paramedics say, "We have a pulse!"

She cried in relief that despite the heartache she was facing, their lives were not lost. She cried for the loss of her relationship and child, and she cried for his betrayal of their love.

Additional LG Chapters

February 2019

- Blindsided by Siera London
- Grace's Revelation by Sydney Aaliyah Michelle
- Crusin' by Celeste Granger
- Wyked by Chelle Ramsey
- Worth the Ride by Hadley Raydeen

October 2018

- Shifting Gears by Olivia Gaines
- Grace's Redemption by Sydney Aaliyah
- Bankrolled by J. L. Campbell
- Riding Dirty by M'Renee Allen
- Freedom by Embue
- Cut: Nationals by Xyla Turner
- Born To Ride by Janae Keyes
- Black Money by Taisha Demay
- The Ultimate Risk by Sheena Binkley

- Justice by Xyla Turner
- Ride for Free by Hadley Raydeen
- Forgiven by Reana Malori
- Onyx Rides by Celeste Granger
- Hampton Roads: Isis by Y. M. Sheree
- Back Off by Toye Lawson Brown

Other Books Written by Celeste:

Samantha McLemore longed to know where she came from; whom she belonged to. Did she have a family? Siblings? What were her parents like? All the questions any child being raised in another family would ask. Of course, Samantha tried to keep moving forward in her life; going to school, earning a degree, attending counseling to deal with the mixed emotions she had about actually finding the people who gave her away. Yet, she felt disconnected; and because of that, struggled to connect, even with the man who claimed to love her. Despite all the challenges, Samantha never stopped. She never gave up the search to find out who she really was.

My Book

One family. Eight sisters tangled in romance. Emery Moore moved away from home after finishing her juris doctorate. She was a successful corporate attorney and had been living in Washington D. C. for the past five years. It wasn't often that she returned home to Atlanta, but the love of her family drew her back. Emery had success in so many facets of her life, but she hadn't been as lucky in love. The word love was unsettling for Emery; it was loaded with notions of submissiveness and sacrifice, the loss of self and being dependent on another person. Notions Emery wasn't sure she wanted. Yet, there was someone Emery couldn't shake her soul loose of, and she tussled with her heart and the sensible tug in her mind daily. Evan Stanton Esq. had been an integral part of Emery Moore's life for the past six months. He like she, was an attorney. During the day, the attorneys at law litigated from different sides of the aisle; fighting with everything they had for their clients. But for the past few months, business was left at the door, and the fighting ended as Evan and Emery delved into uncharted territory. Evan loved how Emery felt in his arms. The curve of her hips, the arch in her back made it difficult to keep his hands off her. It wasn't always like this. Emery had to be pursued, and although Evan was attracted to her unapologetic disposition in the courtroom, along with her sophisticated air, Emery was a challenge; one that Evan planned to take on full steam ahead.

My Book

One family. Eight sisters tangled in romance. Kennedy Moore, the second Moore sister, is the glue that holds the sisterhood together. While Emery, the oldest sister, was away in Washington DC, it was Kennedy that her younger sisters leaned on. A master chef in her own right, Kennedy spends most of her time in the background, pouring her passion into the culinary delicacies she creates for her clientele. Being in the kitchen has left little time for Kennedy to find love, outside of the love she has for culinary arts.

Bryce Monroe is the owner and head chef of Taste, a world-renowned, four-star restaurant in the heart of downtown Atlanta. Much like Kennedy, Bryce spends his days and nights in the kitchen, masterfully creating delectable dishes that keep his clientele coming back for more. Bryce is a multi-millionaire who has everything he's always wanted except someone special to share it with.

An unintentional brush with Bryce Monroe reminds Kennedy that there is more to life than cooking and taking care of her sisters. The two have so much in common, and the chemistry they mutually felt shakes both their foundations. Bryce is captivated by Kennedy and realizes she is what he's been missing. Yet, Kennedy shies away, unsure whether there's room for something more in the world she's created for herself. Will Kennedy let down her guard and allow love in? Will Bryce push past her resistance and pursue the love of his life? Find out in Teach Me Moore: Book 2 in the All That & Moore Series.

Each book in the series is a full novel and can be read as a standalone.

My Book

One family. Eight sisters tangled in romance. Daphne Moore, third eldest sister of the Moore girls, has had tremendous success in her professional life. As the Founder and Head Mistress of Moore Academy for Girls, Daphne taught her girls to be smart, self-reliant and confident. Yet, with all the success in her career, Daphne struggled when it came to matters of the heart. Daphne spent three years of her life loving a man who didn't show the same kind of faithful, unwavering love. The wounds Stephen left were deep, and Daphne wasn't sure she'd ever recover. Nicholas St. John, preeminent real estate developer and multimillionaire, was much like Daphne, successful professionally. However, unlike Daphne, there wasn't an unfaithful lover to taint Nicholas' view on love, Nicholas simply never made time for it. But an accidental encounter between the two would change the trajectory of both their lives.

My Book

One family. Eight sisters, tangled in romance. Felicity

Moore, an actuary, and entrepreneur, deals with facts and numbers as the foundation of her business. Her hard work and nurturing dedication are what makes her a leader in the industry. It's the one thing that her world revolves around on a daily basis, and because of it, there had been no time for love or no place for a relationship in Felicity's life.

It is the sole reason why when Garrett Thompson enters her life, Felicity doesn't take him seriously. Especially with him being a trust fund baby. He's never had to work to earn a living. Although Garrett does dabble in philanthropic endeavors, he spends much of his time living in the lap of luxury; doing the things he wants to and nothing that he doesn't have to. Garrett lives by choice, and any relationship he's had in the past has been an accessory to his lifestyle, not a primary focus. With Garrett living life on his own terms, what if anything do they have in common?

Despite Felicity being dismissive of him, Garrett intends to prove just how serious he can be.

My Book

So many things changed for Samantha McLemore. She found her family, the one she longed for. She found love with Lance Preston, and he loved her without condition despite her brokenness. In an instant, Samantha's life was transformed from barely surviving to living what most would consider a dream life with her multimillionaire fiancé. Still, Samantha was scared; fearful that the love she finally felt in her heart was not real… was undeserved. Would Lance's love be enough? Would Samantha finally feel worthy and truly let love in?

FIND OUT IN I FOUND MOORE. THIS IS A STANDALONE novella.

My Book

He was her best friend. She was the girl of his dreams.
Charity Moore is on the cusp of becoming the neurosurgeon she has always dreamed of becoming. As a student

physician for world-renowned Emory University Hospital, Charity demonstrates her intellectual prowess in the classroom and in the operating room. Charity has been plotting her course of becoming a surgeon for as long as she can remember. She plays by the rules, colors within the lines and does what is necessary to make her dreams come true.

O'Shea Ali is also a student physician at Emory Hospital. As the son of international industry giants, financial security has never been an issue. For O'Shea, becoming a neurosurgeon isn't about prestige or financial gain. His desire stems from O'Shea's passion to charter new medical territory and save lives. O'Shea lives his life passionately without restriction. He fights for what he believes in and is a fierce protector of the ones he loves. That includes Charity.

But emerging desire crosses the friendship line, catapulting Charity and O'Shea out of the friendship zone and into dangerous territory. Charity fears their new entanglement is risky and may cost her the very relationship she treasures most. While O'Shea's unbridled yearnings for Charity become harder to contain, he doesn't want to lose what they have in pursuit of what he craves.

The All That and Moore series follows each sister in the Moore family as they navigate through the entanglements romance brings. Each book can be enjoyed if read as a stand-alone or if it's read in the order of the series

WHEN IS LOVE NOT LOVE? ONYX MALONE, THE OWNER OF Café Laquette, a popular eatery in downtown Atlanta, thought she was in love with Dillon Long, an entrepreneur in his own right. But when the relationship failed, Onyx was prepared to move on. Dillon wasn't. Dillon refuses to let Onyx go, and his definition of love turns ugly. Onyx finds herself on the defense, shadowed and stalked by the man who once claimed undying love for her.

Multimillionaire Egypt Anderson is not only the CEO of his own construction and development company, but he is also the President of the Down South Riders, a motorcycle club. Egypt spends his days in the boardroom and his nights on the back of his classic Harley Davidson. Egypt and Onyx don't travel in the same circles and at first glance, seem to have very little in common. But, a chance encounter with a ruggedly handsome Egypt changes the trajectory of Onyx's life and redefine what love really is.

My Book

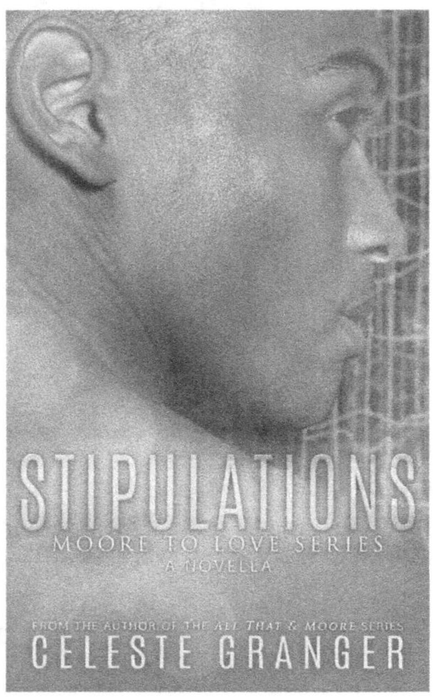

Sloan Moore, a trilingual translator, and communications specialist, proffered her expert services throughout the Southern region, bridging the language gap for business and individuals alike. The one language that Sloan found difficulty speaking was the language of true love. There had been men who entered her life; however, their exit was swift as Sloan struggled to make a real connection with them. Sloan was fiercely independent and unapologetic about the conditions she thought were important to a relationship. She had an amazing career, good friends and a family that loved her. She wasn't looking for anyone to fix or save her.

Titus Phillips, millionaire entrepreneur, and philanthropist have a lot in common. He too was unapologetic about his success, spending his days running a profitable business and his nights doing what any handsome, successful bachelor would do. Titus lived life to the fullest, taking no prisoners in his quest to live every day as though it were his last. Titus balanced his high-octane lifestyle with philanthropic endeavors; giving back whenever he could. A chance encounter brought Sloan into Titus' orbit. The magnetism between the two shifted the earth on its access. Sloan was Titus' to have, only if he could handle the stipulations.

My Book

Their first encounter seemed innocent enough. But fate had other plans. They met on the campus of Jackson State University. She was a freshman. He was an upper-classmen. They fell in love. He broke her heart. Their second encounter could not be so easily dismissed. This time it didn't feel accidental, it felt fated; as though the universe nodded in their direction. Yet past hurts weren't easy to forgive. And sometimes, past loves couldn't be resurrected; nor could they.

Persia Moore was the youngest air traffic controller at

Hartsfield Jackson Airport in Atlanta. She lived for the job and was graceful under pressure. But Persia went home alone every night. During the day, Gabriel Fitzpatrick tended to his million-dollar fortune developing high-end security systems for individuals and businesses alike. At night, Gabriel serenaded the crowds with songs of love and promise. And after that, Gabriel went home alone.

One night, quite by chance, Persia heard Gabriel sing, and nothing would ever be the same again.

This is a second chance romance, standalone, in the Moore to Love series.

My Book

Tempestt Moore, respected curator for a highly successful museum in Atlanta, needed a fantasy when her own love life flatlined. She'd been with Samuel for a few years. He was good to her, provided for her. There was obligatory love but no excitement. Tempestt found that and more at Masquerade.

ALTHOUGH REAL ESTATE MOGUL, XAVIER MALONE, WAS ONE of the most desired bachelors in Atlanta, he spent most of his time managing his passion project, Masquerade. He was all about business until she walked in. Xavier was instantly drawn to her, like a moth to a flame, but his own past held him back and kept him from pursuing the object of his desire.

Can a clandestine encounter truly be a brush with destiny?

FIND OUT IN TEMPTATIONS, BOOK 3 IN THE MOORE TO LOVE Novella Series. This is a standalone novella with a high heat index.

My Book
Find out in I Found Moore. This is a standalone novella.
Coming Soon!

Want to be in the know? Subscribe to my newsletter to be a part of Celeste Granger's Tangled Romance!

https://landing.mailerlite.com/webforms/landing/k2e1j4

Join my Reading Group! https://www.facebook.com/groups/1943300475969127/

Follow me on Facebook @ https://www.facebook.com/TheCelesteGranger/